GOODBYE MERCY

GOODBYE MERCY

... Beyond the region called *Kagawa*,

where the darkness flies low...

Amber Renee'

CHASE 'EM, SELF-PUBLISHING ©2017

AMBER RENEE'

First Edition.

Goodbye Mercy

Renee', Amber. Cover Design: Dean, Cynthia.

2017 by Amber Renee'. All rights reserved.

Dark Fantasy/ Science Fiction/ Young Adult/ Psychology

ISBN # 978-0-9990998-0-3. English.

United States Library of Congress Cataloging (2017 processing)

Chase 'Em, Self-publishing. Amber Renee'.

Other publications by this author:

Owens, Amber. Illustrator: Owens, Nychole.

Babies Come From Where?! © 2015 by Amber Owens. All rights
reserved.

Fantasy/ Science Fiction/ Family/ Humor

ISBN # 978-1-5043-3950-6. English.

United States Library of Congress

Self-published by Amber Owens. Manufactured, printed, distributed by
Balboa Press, a division of Hay House.

GOODBYE MERCY

To the ones who know the dark place – it will be okay!

CHAPTER 1

WARNING: IT WANTS INSIDE

Mercy strips off her jeans in front of the bedroom mirror, and pulls on her running pants. She stretches off her baggy pajama shirt, and pulls on a fitted yellow tank top over her black sports-bra. Combing her feathered strands of silky red hair into an effortless pony-tail with her fingers, she glances in the mirror noticing how the tank top accentuates the sexy curves of her toned body. She self-consciously changes back into the baggy t-shirt to better hide her figure.

Lacing up her tennis shoes, she sighs and whispers to herself,

"I'm gonna break. I can't do it all. There's only so much one person can do... Only so much I can take."

Walking into the living room, she catches sight of Remedy, who sits on the couch watching a documentary. She has her skinny legs wrapped up in a blanket while the air conditioner blows full blast. Her long milk-chocolate brown hair cascades over her shoulders, as she holds a mug of tea with her bone-thin fingers. Engulfed by the movie, Remedy doesn't notice Mercy staring at her in the background.

Mercy loves looking at Remedy. Every time she feels like giving up, like life is just too much to endure, Remedy's effervescent existence reminds her that life has a purpose, a beautiful purpose. Mercy leans over the couch and hugs Remedy from behind, smelling the mango scent of her hair.

"I'm outta here to blow off some steam. Wanna come with?" Mercy asks.

"No thanks. I just settled into a nice cup of chai, and an interesting documentary about McMurdo Dry Valley Antarctica. Thinking about all the cool creatures that can survive on this earth is amazing!" Remedy sips her tea, shaking her head in awe.

Mercy raises her eyebrows and nods her head in slow motion in response to Remedy's goofy excitement. It fascinates Mercy to see her sister's obsession with knowledge, especially about geographical locations.

"Not to mention," Remedy continues, "I'm finishing your speech for the funeral before we head out to Dane's place tonight."

Mercy walks to the front door,

"You're amazing, Rem! Thanks so much for writing that funeral speech for me. I totally buckle up when I think too deeply about all that life and death crap. It's simple: we live or we die. Why do people feel the need to gather together to talk about it? Right? Once we're not breathing, we're just a thing – a dead, lifeless thing. Yet it's supposed to be normal that living people sit around thinking and talking about the dead? Funerals make no sense!"

Remedy enduringly listens to Mercy's morbid rant as she usually does. Once she thinks Mercy has finished, she jokes, "I love how crazy in the coconut you are."

"But really, Rem. Do you get where I'm coming from? It truly makes no sense to think about death, or life for that matter, too deeply. We live, then die – period. Ya get me?"

"Mmh, yea... I get you, sis," Remedy pacifyingly

affirms while sipping her tea.

Mercy notices Remedy quietly looking down into her cup. She knows that indicates that Remedy is not interested in entertaining her line of thinking on the subject anymore. So, she changes the subject,

"Anyhoo. Are you sure you don't wanna come?"

"Eh, no thanks. You know me: I'd rather work my brain than my body any day. I practice the power of the imagination, ever since that documentary I told you about a while ago that proved how people can literally think their way into great health with minimal physical exertion... Yea, that's pretty much the route I choose to take. But you go ahead. Have fun."

"Oki doki, Einstein. Work your brain, while I work my heart."

"Got your mace, right?"

"As always," she reassures Remedy, raising the mace bottle in the air. She opens the front door, "Love you. Be back in a while."

"Ok. Love you, too. Be careful, Mer."

Mercy stands outside on the front porch of their townhouse for a moment to admire the hilltop view overlooking the university campus that she and Remedy attend. She breathes in deeply through her nose, feeling the inhaled oxygen circulate within her chest. Then she breathes out through her mouth, pushing the air through her lungs, releasing the tension in her body.

Stretching her arms and legs to prepare for the run, she thinks to herself: *One day soon - no more stress. No more demands. No more bad dreams or empty memories. No more overwhelming pain.*

She begins to jog towards the nature park, which is about a mile from her home. Feeling the summer breeze blow warm kisses all over her body, she decides to take the scenic route through campus. She jogs under the archway of the University Science Library.

The archway is lined with imported red brick, engraved with images supposedly dating back thousands of years. Tree branches hang low at each entrance of the tunnel. They weave into each other, blocking the sunlight like umbrellas, creating a cave effect. Birds of various species flutter secretly among the vines, unknowingly dropping feathers on those who pass underneath.

Mercy exits off University grounds, and returns to the main trail leading to the park. Just as she gets into her favorite part of the park, where the flat terrain elevates and merges into an antiquated bridge, a man in the near distance distracts her focus.

He sits alone on one of the few benches in the park with his head hunched over, wearing a uniquely textured black trench coat. The leather textured material stretches tightly over his body, as if the coat is too small for his thick build which protrudes from underneath.

With his back facing Mercy as she approaches, she notices his body squirming strangely, like he's attempting to get comfortable. She assumes that his standing height probably reaches about seven feet because sitting down he's at least her height. As she gets closer, she hears his shrilling voice,

"It's her, it's her! I know, I told you it's her. She's

coming."

She approaches with trepidation, wondering what he's talking about, and why in the world he is wearing a full-length black coat in the middle of summer. She gets a creepy feeling from him, but isn't about to let some random coo-coo take her out of her exercise zone.

In Mercy's usual hot-tempered fashion, she begins to *wish* he messes with her! Then she can take out her frustrations on him. The frustrations of unfair tribulations... of mundane life. Of unreachable education, of pointless work, of fleeting pleasures, and of permanent struggles.

Of feeling tired of being tired. Exacerbated by all the strenuous efforts to be a positive person, despite most people not giving a care about reciprocating positivity. Feeling exhausted from possessing optimistic endurance through seemingly never-ending obstacles and disappointments. Only for such endurance to ultimately lead to meaningless victories.

Not to mention, the pain of losing loved ones in death. Like how Dane, her best friend, just lost his dad, who was also like *her* dad. A rare man full of genuine love and generous kindness. The only dad she's ever known. The only adult who guided her and supported her for more than half of her life, and never expected anything in return. A man joyously grateful for a simple "thank you."

She loved him because he was one reason in life to believe that she wasn't alone... that a stranger could love deeper than a close blood relative. Dane begged her to speak at the funeral. She accepted, feeling honored that he asked her to speak on behalf of such a valued person. But as the funeral gets nearer, she doesn't want to uphold the commitment anymore.

She feels that attachments only expose her vulnerabilities, causing emotions to bubble out that she'd rather keep bottled up inside. Bottled up to explode in moments like this one in the park, when she illogically thinks a random person is trying to scare her out of finishing her much needed evening run.

Bring it on dude, because I'm in just the right mood to get crazy right back at you if that's what you're planning, she says to herself about the wiggling guy in the trench coat. She grips her bottle of mace and attempts to pass him as swiftly as possible, knowing deep down that she really doesn't want to give or receive any more negativity right now. She imagines what Remedy would tell her in this moment:

"Think happy, loving thoughts to raise your energy level and strengthen your resolve to create a positive outcome."

Mercy repeats this in her head with each step towards the man on the bench in the black coat. She finally passes him. He never lifts his crouching head to turn around and look at Mercy.

After passing, she discreetly looks back, curious to see what the face of the strange voice in the trench coat looks like. When she looks back, however, nobody is there.

She stops completely, and looks around in confusion. If he retreated, she would have seen him walking away from the bench – it's a totally open area. "I must really be losing it," she softly says out loud.

Dumbfounded by where the man could have gone that fast, she contemplates whether to finish the route or turn back home to avoid any other strange things from happening. She decides to keep briskly jogging over the bridge.

Clear creek water rushes under the bridge creating background music for the creatures in the bushes and trees that match the sound of her movement. The bridge inclines into a dirt path at the top of the park, where she stops for a rest. She appreciates the glowing ball of fire floating beyond the mountains, turning burnt orange in preparation to set in the pink sky. She hears a large rustle in the piled heap of prehistoric sized branches below.

Not expecting to see much, she looks down into the natural ditch for any interesting animals. But everything instantly seems eerily still. A dark shadow sneaks near. She's startled until she realizes it's just her own shadowy profile created by the falling sun in the distance.

Considering her jarred nerves, and the gradual disappearance of the sunlight, she decides to turn back home now. Plus, she forgot her glasses and can barely see two feet in front of her without them, especially at night.

She jogs down the hill, over the bridge, and back through the park trail. Still no sign of the interesting man in the coat. She does notice, however, a massive tree standing at the entrance of the park, one that she's somehow never noticed before. Compelled to stop at it, she realizes that it's a man-made tree, much taller than the surrounding organic trees.

Its engineers tried to blend it in with the park, with its fake climbing branches and fake green leaves emerging from the metal base of a trunk. But it doesn't blend in because there are no insects crawling on it, no birds perched on its limbs, and no scent of bark expelled from its base. The animals aren't fooled, that's why they stay away from it.

Mercy touches the fake trunk and feels a vibration from inside. Her hand print uncovers some dust revealing a spot with a number, a bar-code. The illegible numbers have been vandalized as if some sharp object intended to completely scratch off the existence of the tree's identification.

"Hunh, that's interesting. It seems like this 'tree' literally just sprung up outta nowhere, but was already vandalized."

She wipes off the dust from her hand onto her pants, and steps back to get one final look at the giant metal tree. Shaking her head in disappointment of this monstrosity of an object, she continues on-route back home.

While she runs, she deeply ponders why humans feel the need to put up giant fake objects. Why not leave nature alone? Why tear down nature only to replace it with repulsive objects of emptiness?

Running up the hill a couple blocks from her neighborhood, she sees a small van parked in the dirt along the sidewalk covered with a tarp. The crinkling sound of the material's subtle movement in the breeze gives her the chills. She does not want to pass too closely to the tented vehicle, so she glances at the other side of the street for an alternate route. Ironically, concrete construction blocks the adjacent sidewalk.

With no other immediate option, she continues jogging forward, passing the tented van. The breeze puffs up the tent, then lets it down again, like it's breathing. Mercy tries to avoid looking because she has a daunting feeling, but glances at it as she passes.

She discerns a shadow underneath the tarp. At first, she guesses it's just the outline of the vehicle, but when it moves at the top, she knows it's not. Without thinking, she impulsively stops to examine the moving shadow underneath the tent. It stops, too. Another gust of wind blows up a portion of the tarp, giving Mercy a better glimpse of what sits underneath.

A dark silver body of some sort crouches still, like a giant metallic statue with layers of intricate armor. The tarp drops back down on the figure but puffs up at the end closest to Mercy. She can't breathe when she witnesses gigantic round yellow eyes examining her.

The tent falls back down, covering the giant creature again.

It was never a van at all. The tarp breathes along with the creature, up and down. Mercy cannot breathe.

"Run, Mer," she commands herself in a low tone. "Get out of here, now!"

In shock, she slowly takes a few steps backwards before she fully turns around and breaks away. As she sprints, she replays in her mind what just happened. The weirdo on the park bench, the nest ditch, the vibrating fake tree, and whatever that was under the tarp. She wonders why she always seems to find the strangest situations... or maybe they always find her.

Loud rustling from behind interrupts her meditative thoughts. Her heart pounds. She spins around in a fright with her finger on the mace trigger.

But nobody is there. She swallows hard and tastes a hint of blood from her boiling lungs. She peers down the dark corridor of desolate road with its abandoned sidewalks and wild bushes.

The wall-sized bush to her left shakes, making her jump to the right. She can't see anything but she hears what sounds like a cat hiss. She reasons it must be a cat, but doesn't wait to find out. She proceeds to run on.

Running again at a swift, steady pace, she still hears the same loud rustling very close behind her. More than hearing it, though, she *feels* something following her. But she can't look back. She feels too scared to see what is hunting her. She picks up speed as she turns the corner of her neighborhood, and simultaneously reaches in her pocket to grab her phone – she forgot that, too.

Then she feels something sharp give her a hard push on the back, making her fall to the concrete. She stumbles and rolls to the ground, feeling her skin scrape open. She quickly looks back to catch a glimpse of the attacker, but all she sees is a very blurry tall and husky body.

She can't make out any details. It just looks like a shadow figure in the darkness of nightfall. She knows it's there, but at the same time she feels unsure of whether it's *really* there.

She crawls away a couple feet on her hands and knees, then turns around and sits on her bottom, leaning back on her palms. He hovers at her feet silently. He's obviously analyzing her - she can feel it.

The image still looks very dark and blurry, so she blinks fast and squints in attempt to clearly see who - or what - it is. She recognizes the black leather coat wrapped tightly around his body.

Then she hears that familiar shrilly voice say,

"I only want what's within you. Just let me take it ... You need me to."

Mercy can't even scream because she's so scared. She notices that his body slowly begins to lift, floating a few inches off the ground. As he starts to spread his arms to open his coat, an unusually loud thumping sound from afar punctures the silent air. He lowers his arms, re-wrapping his body, and swiftly turns to the side as if hearing his name called by someone. He stares motionless into the black distance.

While he's distracted, Mercy searches around in the dark for the mace she dropped on the ground during the fall. She finds it. Fumbling to adjust the latch on the bottle, she looks up and points her weapon, only to discover that he's gone... that instantly and that quietly.

In a panic, she looks all around herself with blurry vision, only to see a desolate road and overgrown bushes on the deserted sidewalks. Without delay, she springs up onto her feet, and proceeds on her quest home, sprinting like there's no tomorrow. Finally reaching her apartment, she burros through the front door, catching Remedy off guard.

"What the heck are you doing, Mercy? What's wrong?"

Mercy slams the door, locks it, then leans up against it panting for breath.

"A guy... a guy was chasing me... whew, hold on," Mercy jogs over to the couch and sits next to Remedy.

Remedy hands Mercy her mug of tea, "Here, take a swig. Catch your breath so you can tell me what in the world happened."

Mercy sips the tea, "Ewe, this tastes gross... it's cold. I thought it was hot tea."

"Well, it *was* hot tea when I made it about an hour ago, but now it's cold. Anyway, what happened?"

"Ok, so there was some guy on a bench in a long trench coat talking to himself out loud when I first got to the bridge. Then he disappeared after I ran passed him. Literally, I looked back and he was gone. Ok, then fast-forward to after that..."

Mercy rolls her fists over each other to illustrate fast-forwarding her story,

"There was the biggest animal that I've ever seen in my life, hiding under a tent on the road. It was just looking at me in the dusk with huge yellow eyes, kind of as if it was waiting for me. So, I ran the heck out of there. Then that's when the guy from the bench, well I think it was *him*, chased me down the street and pushed me to the ground.

And said some crazy stuff about 'wanting to take what's inside of me.' I was like..."

She and Remedy say in sync, "...*Whaaa*?"

"Yea, exactly," Mercy continues. "I couldn't see him clearly though because I forgot my glasses."

Remedy interrupts,

"How many times do I remind you to take your glasses, and you get upset at me. The one time I let you walk outta here for an evening run without saying anything, you forget them."

"Ok, ok, ok. This story isn't about you being right, Rem. It's about the weirdo who basically told me that he's going to murder me. And all you're worried about is

30

saying 'I told you so' about my glasses."

Remedy just shakes her head and bites her tongue, considering she's not the argumentative type. Mercy continues to bicker for a moment, however, because she *is* the argumentative type.

"I storm into the house with cuts and bruises, saying a guy is out to get me, and you're talking about glasses. Not the fact that there was a giant creature stalking me. Or that someone slammed me to the ground and said he wants to slice me open. No ... glasses." Mercy raises both her hands in the air, "Is whether or not I had my glasses really the crucial part of the story?"

Remedy says nothing but makes a circling gesture with her hand to incite Mercy to continue with the story.

"Anyway, when I went to spray him with the mace, he was gone. I didn't see him or even hear him leave. Seems like I would have, especially because he was only a few feet away from me. Plus, he was a big dude! I'd guess way over six feet tall, thick built, long black thin-leather coat... easy to distinguish if he ran away. So, I would've seen him running. But, nope, the street was empty both ways. Didn't see or hear anything. It was just like poof – he was gone."

"Ok, so you called the police, right?"

Mercy was dreading that question because she didn't want to admit that she forgot her phone, too.

"Or did you forget your phone, too, since I didn't remind you of that either when you left?"

Mercy's ears turn tomato red from embarrassment,

"Look, the important thing is that I'm safely home now. I don't want to call the police and make a big deal of it. I'm fine. We don't have time for that anyway. I just want to hop in the shower, and get to the airport to catch our flight to Dane's."

"Uh... I think you should call the police if some crazy person is wandering about out there attacking people. Not to mention, some unidentified creature lurking in darkness, waiting for people. I would call if that all happened to me."

Mercy shakes her head "no" at Remedy. One part of her wants to report everything to prevent anyone else from getting hurt, but the other part doesn't want to sound crazy. After all, she is still uncertain herself of exactly what she saw.

"OK, that's on *your* conscience, I guess," Remedy adds, "Are you sure you're ok, though?"

"It's fine. I'm fine. Let's change the subject now," she answers, hiding her shaken nerves.

Mercy walks to the kitchen. She gulps down a fresh cup of water and scarfs down a cold piece of left-over fried chicken. With her mouth full, she asks,

"Did you finish the speech for me?"

"Yep. It's all set and ready to go. I tried to think morbid like you so that it would sound like your words, and hopefully, makes you feel more comfortable reading it aloud."

"Cool, thanks! Alright, I'll be outta the shower in a few."

"Ok. Then we need to get a move on 'cause it's getting late."

Entering the bathroom, Mercy rubs her neck and stares up at the ceiling for a moment, wishing she could run away from life. Peering into the wooden-framed mirror over the pedestal sink, she smiles at her reflection, but her eyes don't sparkle, and the corners of her lips aren't lifted by happy cheeks. A forced smile without meaning ... what everyone in the world is used to. Tears fill her eyes, then stream down her cheeks.

She doesn't understand how she can feel totally strong one minute, and the next, feel like crumbling for no apparent reason. Today's tears could be from unsettled nerves caused by the strange encounters while running. Spontaneous situations often trigger dormant emotions, even unrelated ones. Or maybe there's a deeper issue ... she doesn't know what makes her change so fast.

She cradles her face in her hands and begins to cry more. Remedy hears Mercy crying from the living room. She runs to the bathroom door, and sees Mercy sitting on the floor, broken and sobbing with her head in her hands. She immediately kneels next to her sister and embraces her with all her might.

"Mer? Are you ok? What's wrong?" She wipes Mercy's

tears sympathetically and kisses her forehead.

Mercy can't bring herself to respond right away. Finally, she sniffles and says,

"I don't know ... I just feel ... angry ... and sad ... which makes me angrier that I'm so sad. I'm angry that there are weirdo people out in the world doing whatever they want, yet good people are dying. I'm sad that people die at all. I'm angry over things I can't control. I feel sad that every time I think about death, I wonder if our parents are dead ... and I hate wondering about our parents."

She looks up at Remedy, revealing angry red veins of hurt in her eyes,

"... Then that makes me have to consciously think about how we don't even KNOW our parents ... or any of our relatives for that matter. It's like, why care about trying to find anything positive about life when there's always negativity? Not just negativity from outside, but from within. It's just all too overwhelming, ya know? Makes me start wishing *I* was dead, or at least was never born."

Remedy pushes Mercy's head down onto her chest and holds her. In a soothing motherly voice, Remedy attempts to offer consolation,

"Don't talk like that. What happened during your run just creeped you out, and triggered all these random emotions. I understand how you feel, but you should ignore those disturbing thoughts. Don't dwell on wanting to die. That'll only cause more depression. Try to find why you desire to live instead of focusing on why you want to die ... even if it's only one reason – hang on to that one reason with all you've got."

She squeezes Mercy, and Mercy hugs back.

"One day, we'll find our family, Mer. And even if we never do, and it's only us two forever, is that so bad? Don't worry. One day, it'll all be easier."

"When?"

"When it's over. In the meantime, you don't have to be miserable in your thoughts. Just change how you see things, and the things you choose to see will change."

Mercy nods her head in submissive agreement, and

wipes her nose on her sleeve.

"Now I know you must be feeling bad because you, Miss Germaphobe, just wiped your nose into your sleeve instead of into a tissue."

Mercy laughs at Remedy's disgusted reaction, then quickly tries to put her infested sleeve on Remedy's face. Remedy scoots back and screams, forcefully grabbing Mercy's arm.

"D-O-N'-T you dare, Mercy! I'm not kidding!"

They struggle playfully.

"Who's the germaphobe now, Rem?"

"C'mon, Mer! That's gross!"

Mercy accidentally slips on the bath mat, and falls flat onto Remedy, knocking the wind out of them both. She quickly rolls off Remedy, onto the floor.

When she sees Remedy frantically checking her face and shirt, she bursts out laughing. Remedy laughs, too. Thankfully, she's not the kind of person to take herself too seriously. She finds it beautiful that Mercy is cracking up now instead of crying. Mercy sits up and leans against the bathtub. She and Remedy pause in loving silence.

Mercy stands up and straightens her oversized shirt over her thighs. Remedy reaches out her hand for Mercy to pull her up, and accidentally static-shocks Mercy. Mercy wiggles her fingers,

"Yikes, Rem! Why do you do that almost every time?"

"Sorry, sorry, sorry!"

They stand in front of each other, practically mirror images. Hands on their hips, they look at each other like, *Whelp, glad that sad moment is over.*

"You alright?" Remedy asks.

"Yup. Just the usual random emotional break-down, that's all. But I'm all good now."

"I'm always here for you, Mer. You know that, right?"

"I do. And I'm here for you, too."

They hug, and do their secret childhood hand shake by slapping each other's hands twice then locking pinky fingers. Remedy leaves Mercy to finish getting dressed in the bathroom.

After finishing, Mercy meets Remedy at the car, who waits in the driver seat rummaging through her music to play for the night's short road trip. After loading up the trunk, Mercy hops in the passenger seat, unaware that the giant silver stalker watches in the dark. They drive off to a secluded airport where Dane has arranged for a private plane to pick them up.

CHAPTER 2

WARNING: THE SKY

They drive in the black of the summer's night with their windows cracked. Mercy admires the stillness of the crisp air. She catches sporadic sounds from the nocturnal creatures outside who are probably watching them as they pass. There are no cars, no lights on the two-lane mountain highway, and no noises except for the spurts of animal creeks from within the hills. Tonight appears unusually dark, or perhaps it's just the reason for the trip that makes it feel dark.

"So, have you talked to Dane today, Mer?"

"No, I just texted him that we're on our way to the airport. I talked to him yesterday, though," Mercy answers, biting into a stick of string cheese. "He tried to explain how he feels. He doesn't really express himself to anyone but me, so he kinda unloads his feelings on me. It's a little much sometimes. But thankfully he knows that about me... that I can get overloaded with emotions because I soak in other people's pain on top of my own. I appreciate how unselfish he is to give me space when I need it, even when he's going through a lot."

"Poor fella! He's the sweetest guy ever. It's very uncommon to find one like him who is caring, kind, strong, smarty pants, Mister rich engineer... **and** he's freaking CuTe! I know you've told me so many times before, but why exactly haven't you snagged him yet? Because sistah, if you don't soon, *I* will."

"Simmer down, Rem." Mercy pats Remedy on the head. "All those things you listed are all the exact reasons why we'll probably never get together. He's ... *perfect*. We're too opposite. He's calm, I'm the master of panic. He's patient, I hate waiting. He's strong, I'm weak. He's smart, and I'm smarter..."

Remedy and Mercy giggle together at Mercy's slip of feminine cockiness.

"... Seriously, though. He engineers inanimate objects. I engineer living things: organisms and cells. Obviously, no comparison there of who's a tad more genius."

They chuckle again together.

She continues,

"But he is very smart, I'll hand that to him. That reminds me of another thing: he's so hard-working and rigid. I'm only studying science because I love it... I feel happy getting lost in all the details of the mysterious. But I don't even care about a prestigious position in society, which is why I likely won't even pursue a career in it. Watch, I'll end up working at a zoo or something."

"Yea, I could see you end up doing something like that. But as far as the 'oppositions' between you and Dane: those are all things you can deal with, Mer, trust me. Those aren't deal breakers."

"Ok, fine. What about the fact that I'm an orphan without any family, except my sister, while he's surrounded by family galore?"

Remedy quickly replies, "His family **is** your family. They've taken you and me both in as their own. Dane has proven that he doesn't care at all about your family background or lack thereof, and that he wants to give you a stable family."

Mercy massages her shoulders, uncomfortable with the thought of family. She slyly shifts the conversation to a lighter note,

"Ok. Well, what about the fact that he loves being around people, and I'm a recluse? He'd be miserable having to be alone with me most of the time because I wouldn't want to ever leave the house."

Remedy puts one hand on her cheek and mockingly makes a sad face,

"Oh, he'd be **so** miserable in the house with his dream girl all to himself. Whatever would he find to do if he had you *all alone, all the time*?"

Mercy gives Remedy a gentle nudge on the side of her head.

"That's gross, Rem. I don't think of him like that."

"You mean to tell me you *never* thought of him like

that before? With his naturally sculpted body, clean-cut style, and exotically handsome face? In all this time that you guys have been best friends for over 10 years, and he's always been in love with you? Even when he was with 'what's-her-face,' you know he was still loving his little Mercy. The way he practically drools over you every time he's near you, doesn't get your blood boiling just a little? Yeah, right! You guys are meant for each other."

Mercy bashfully looks down at her lap because she knows it's true. The light from the car radio screen highlights her pink jeans in the dark car.

"Well... I do hope that one day..." she begins to admit to the tingles she reciprocally feels for Dane, but a flash of light from the sky distracts her,

"...Oh my goodness!" Mercy points her finger on the window, "Rem, look at those falling stars!"

Remedy leans forward and looks up through the windshield. They are both mesmerized to see masses of colorful blazing trails flashing in the sky. The more stars that appear, the more the sky lights up, coloring the road and hills surrounding them. It brings an instant sense of mystical adventure.

"I've never seen anything like this before. Have you?"

"No. It's absolutely breath-taking. I love stars! Hurry, Mer, take a picture of it! Hurry!"

Remedy continues to look up at the sky while driving along the dark strip of road, concluding that it's safe since no other cars are on the road anyway. Mercy tries to capture the star show but can't get a good shot.

"Let's stop, Rem. Pull over. I'll get better pictures that way."

When Remedy redirects her focus on the road, she screams and slams on the brakes. Mercy whips her head around to face the front of the car. She gets a glimpse of why Remedy screamed, seeing a terrifying image preparing to smash into the windshield. They both take cover with their arms over their faces to protect themselves from the effects of the crash. The car stops.

After a moment, they unravel from their protective positions to assess the damage. To their surprise, there is no shattered glass and no apparent damage to the car. The David Bowie CD continues to play music in the background as they sit frightened in a silent daze, unsure of what they just saw colliding into the headlights.

"Did you see that, Mercy?"

"I don't know what I just saw. I could've sworn it was an owl. But like a HUGE owl... it's impossible for a bird's head to be almost the size of the whole windshield ... riiiiight???"

Remedy nervously floods out words in a fast, high-pitched voice,

"I would think so, but I'm pretty sure I saw a big owl, too. That's why I screamed because its wings were literally longer than the width of the car, and it was flying straight into the car. That was so spooky! I *had* to have hit it. That was a head-on collision. But there's no shattered glass. And I didn't feel an actual hit. Did you?"

"Nope, I didn't either. That's really weird."

In simultaneous harmony, they look at each other and ask,

"Should we get out and look?"

Mercy admits, "I don't really want to, but if you want..." She pauses, and from anxious habit begins to nibble on her fingernails.

Remedy first flashes the bright lights to examine the road through the windshield from inside the car. "I don't really want to get out either. But I would feel so bad if I started driving and ran over it. I'll just get out real quick and look. Watch my back."

Apprehensively, Remedy gets out leaving her door open and walks to the front of the car. Mercy immediately leans over and pulls the door closed. Remedy looks back at her like, *What the heck are you doing*? And Mercy returns a look like, *I'm not leaving the door open so a giant owl can get inside the car with me*!

Mercy watches Remedy scurry all around the outside of the car. Remedy hurriedly climbs back into the driver's seat and locks the door.

"There's nothing out there. And the car doesn't even have a dent or scratch. How weird!"

Still biting her nails down to the nubs, Mercy ponders out loud, "Seems like something of that magnitude would have at least left a scratch. We had to have hit it..."

Remedy shrugs, "Oh well."

"Don't you have a weird feeling right now, Rem? It's like we're clear on what just happened and what we saw, but it feels like it might not have happened at all. Kind of like, we know what we were *supposed* to see, but maybe it wasn't actually there."

Remedy presses the automatic door lock again and looks in the rear-view mirror,

"I'm getting freaked out, so let's not talk about it ever again or even think about it anymore."

She presses heavy on the gas pedal, and cranks up the music to avert any further discussion of it. As they drive off through the dark mountain, Mercy can't stop thinking about what they could have seen and why they feel so strange about the experience.

Road kill without the kill. Very strange. And the star show faded away without them consciously noticing it, leaving the sky a black canvas of sparse twinkles.

Reaching the guarded gate to the private airport, Remedy gives the guard their confirmation code and ID cards. He speaks into his security phone, which acts as a two-way radio, and another voice answers back. The gate opens for Remedy to drive through. She parks the car in an isolated hangar, then they walk to the landing area a short distance away.

Soon after, a small plane lands on the mountain strip. The engine quiets and the door opens. Out walks a guy, tall and very impressive in appearance. Mercy runs over to him,

"Dane! I didn't know you were gonna come. I thought you were just sending the plane for us."

Dane smiles big at the sight of Mercy. The lights from the plane reflect off his copper-colored eyes making them look like shiny new pennies. He carries himself modestly and unassumingly. One would never guess that he's loaded with cash or extremely educated. His flawless smile is welcoming, his sparkling eyes are honest, and his presence is humble.

"Of course, I came! I wouldn't leave you and Rem to fly in all by yourselves."

They warmly embrace, while Remedy quietly stands back and observes how he closes his eyes and breathes in the scent of Mercy's skin. He glances up and realizes Remedy watching his enamored trance.

"Hey!" He says to Remedy, gently letting go of Mercy to give Remedy a brief hug around the neck like an old buddy, old pal. He runs his fingers through his messy beach-style curls,

"Good to see you, Remy. How was your drive?"

Remedy quickly answers before Mercy starts running her mouth about the illogical encounter with the unexplained giant bird. "It was fine. We're happy it wasn't too long of a trip."

She cuts a threatening look at Mercy, denoting not to talk about the unsettling experience. Mercy sticks her tongue out at Remedy.

Remedy nods her head and mumbles, "That's right."

"Ok," Dane chimes in, "I feel totally out of the loop. This is either an inside joke between sisters **or** something crazy happened on the way here that you're trying to hide. Either way, I'm staying out of it," Dane surrenders the conversation by putting his hands up.

They all board the plane and settle in as it takes off towards the remote area where Dane lives. Unbeknownst to them, rolls of fluffy neon pink waves of clouds swirl under the plane like a violent ocean torrent in the dark night's sky. Splashes of clouds disperse upwards around the plane, like tiny spherical mushroom clouds, turning a purplish black as they disseminate ...

And the giant white owl wisps in and out of the clouds, stalking the plane closely.

CHAPTER 3

WARNING: AT AN ODD HOUR

When the plane lands, and the door opens, they see a field of mist crawling over red rock. Water spouts toss up crystal clear water. Green patches of healthy grass shine from the road lights leading up to Dane's mansion. The lights also illuminate the sign that says:

Fly Geyser, Nevada – **Private Property**

As well as other signs that warn against tourists and sightseers.

"I would love to live here," Mercy says in a low voice as she walks out behind Dane.

"Don't worry. I'm sure you'll probably be moving here one day soon, sis," Remedy elbows Mercy and winks. Mercy slaps her arm.

Dane turns back, "What happened?"

"Nothing," they both mischievously answer together.

A white car pulls up, and escorts them up the hill to the front steps of Dane's home. They notice a ton of cars parked in the small parking lot. Knowing their hesitation to enter a house full of his relatives, Dane assures them,

"A lot of people are already asleep. But if you don't mind just saying a quick 'hello' to my mom, she'd appreciate that. She's waiting up to see you guys. Oh yeah, and I reserved the guest house for you guys. You won't have to stay in the main house, having to talk to everyone all weekend."

Mercy and Remedy take a sigh of relief, and follow Dane up the porch stairs and into the house. About 10 relatives are still awake in the main family room looking at pictures and drinking wine while music plays low in the background. As they enter, Dane's mom, Connie, runs over to welcome them.

"My girls!" Connie proudly says taking a hand from each of them. "It's been too long, my little beauties. Come in and get comfortable."

Dane places their bags in the kitchen near the back door which leads to the guest house. Connie introduces the girls to everyone. One little lady stands up, puts her hand out, and says,

"I'm Jewel. We've never met before."

They each reluctantly shake hands with her, knowing that they've met her plenty of times. In fact, she's the relative they've seen the most out of everybody (besides Dane's parents).

Mercy confirms, "Oh... actually we have met."

Both Remedy and Mercy add in sync, "You don't remember us?"

"Whoa, you guys talk the same, and look the same, too."

Mercy answers, "Well, that's because we're twins."

"Really? I would've remembered meeting twins. Are you sure you're twins? Have you been twins the whole time?"

Remedy and Mercy look at each other, holding back

laughter, then look back at Jewel.

"Yea," Remedy answers. "Pretty sure we've always been twins since the day we were born. The only real difference is our hair color."

Jewel points at Remedy's body, "And that you don't like to eat."

"Oh wow," Connie intervenes. "Jewel, that's – uh – kind of rude."

Remedy timidly attempts to lighten the moment, "Oh, it's ok."

Everyone looks around at each other, awkwardly uncomfortable. Then, off a tangent, Jewel asks,

"So, did you guys arrive safely?"

"Um, are you asking if we had any trouble getting here?" Mercy asks.

"No. I'm asking if you're here safely?"

Mercy feels her ears turn red from irritation, now fed up with Jewel's conversation. Sensing this, Remedy steps in to answer before Mercy says something offensive.

"Yea, we're here safely ... that's how we're standing here, right in front of you."

"Oh, good because I was so worried! Ooooh, now I remember you two! You're the orphan twins ..."

Dane cuts her off,

"... Ok, ok, ok. We've gotta get these ladies to bed. So, I'm gonna walk them over to the guest house. Good night everyone."

While they walk through the courtyard to the guest house, Dane apologizes for that incident. Mercy and Remedy shrug it off like no big deal. Aroma of jasmine flowers and orange blossoms sweetly flavor the air in the courtyard. Entering the guest house, they observe the pure glass wall of the living room and kitchen, which displays an outside waterfall. Mercy walks straight to the kitchen to start an investigation of inventory.

Dane exclaims, "Yes – the kitchen is stocked! I already

knew you'd go straight for the goods."

She pulls out a piece of string cheese from the refrigerator, "Yay!"

Remedy heads to her room, "I'm pooped. I'm gonna jump in the shower and knock out. Good night guys!"

"Night," Dane and Mercy both reply.

Mercy begins to pull out the freshly cut fruit and cold fried chicken from the fridge. "You know me so well, Dane! Yummy yummy!"

Dane sits at the bar, astutely watching Mercy eat enthusiastically.

"I love seeing you happy, Mer."

She looks up with her mouth full and grins at him. She feels her body tingle when they lock eyes. Self-conscious that she probably looks like a wreck, tired and stuffing her face, she deflects,

"How do you feel? Are you ready for tomorrow?"

"I still can't believe Doc is gone," he rubs his eyes trying to stop the tears that want to fall. "You know how you've always told me that you wouldn't mind dying? Just to fall asleep one night and never wake up because of the unbearable reality that you can't escape your own crippling thoughts? Well, now I finally understand that feeling."

He keeps his eyes closed, covering them with his fingers as he speaks. She chews laboriously while listening.

"I never understood you before, Mer. I couldn't understand how anyone could feel that hopeless... that lost... that unimportant. But now I understand."

He runs his fingers from his eyes, up his forehead and through his curls. When he opens his eyes, they flicker and push out sad flowing tears that match the background glass wall with the flowing waterfall outside.

Mercy stares back at him, her own tears now fall heavily and abruptly from feeling his pain. She adds,

"It's like... you just want everyone to go away, so that you can be alone ... so that there's nothing left that's valuable to fight for. Then it can all end because you can finally let go. Right?"

He looks down at the counter and nods.

"I'm sorry, Dane. I wouldn't wish this emotional battle on my worst enemy, let alone someone I ..." she pauses, "... I love."

Although he is still looking down, she sees him smile. She bites her thumb nail nervously, waiting for him to say something. He looks up and says,

"Doc left a gift for you and Rem."

He places a blue memory stick on the table.

"He always remembered how you wanted to find your relatives. So, he did some extensive research for you, and found some info. It's all on here. He kept it a secret, so I don't know what's there."

Her jaw drops. She covers her mouth with both hands to conceal her excitement which seems unfitting in the moment.

"He intended to actually find any of your living relatives in person and do a whole surprise party type thing, but... well... he ran outta time, I guess."

She somberly walks around the counter and just stands in front of him, not sure of exactly what to say or do. He grabs her waist, and buries his face in her belly. Tightly tugging at the sides of her shirt, he belts out a cry. She wraps her arms around his shoulders and massages his soft curls, as her own shedding tears dampen the back of his shirt.

After a couple minutes, she hears him say, "I love you."

She's unsure if he said that in reply to her earlier expression, or if he's rhetorically speaking out loud to the memory of his dad. He pulls away and wipes his tears. Reaching in his pocket, he pulls out an envelope.

"And this is also for you... you and Remy."

He hands it to her. Inside is a note that simply says,

"My baby girls, I'll forever watch over you. Love, Doc."

Behind the note, she unfolds a monetary check from Lewis Krete Troy (Dane's dad), made out to: Mercy Fox

Kagawi and/or Remedy Loyal Kagawi, in an amount that will take care of them both for the rest of their lives.

She holds the check to her heart and closes her eyes,

"Thank you, Doc. I wish I could thank you one more time for loving me."

She feels Dane's hand sweep her hair behind her ear. She opens her eyes.

"He knows you were thankful. That's why he wanted you to have that. He distributed all his money very selectively during his final days. Only a few of us were discreetly left with an amount like yours because he didn't want people fighting over money in the event of his death. The bulk went to charities, orphanages, homeless shelters, and such. He wanted to make sure people knew there wasn't any more money left to hassle us for."

He kisses her forehead, and walks to the door.

"Sleep tight, Mer. We'll be leaving about 9 AM. Oh yeah, and you're going to give your speech after my

Uncle Les speaks. I can't wait to hear what you'll say to remember Doc. Good night."

As she stands there, stomach full, check in hand, in the middle of this beautiful guest house surrounded by people who love her, she realizes how much she has to be grateful for. And in this moment, this sad moment, she paradoxically feels overjoyed.

After changing into her pajamas, she puts the zip drive next to the printer on the desk. She's eager to know what information was gathered. Although she's so tempted to learn whatever is contained in those papers, she feels like she would be betraying Remedy to read it without her knowledge. So she prints out the information without reading it. She leaves the printed pages on the glass-top desk to go over with Remedy the next night.

She lies down in the bed, unable to sleep because of the dead-silence. She stares up at the ceiling fan near the skylight. She turns on the fan with the remote control, and closes her eyes. All is quiet, except for the whisper from the ceiling fan.

She opens her eyes, and quickly clicks the off button.

No more whisper. Her heart pounds. She keeps her eyes open and turns on the fan again as a test. The whisper hisses out louder than before, but the words are unclear. She hurries to turn it off, and leaves it off.

From the living room, a clicking sound echoes in the silence. It reminds her of bird feet tapping on glass. After several minutes of calming herself down, her tension finally eases. Her eyes become heavy and her body feels like it's sinking into the mattress. She enters her dream...

Standing at the kitchen sink, washing dishes, Mercy accidentally drops a glass and it breaks. She gathers the broken pieces of glass as if she is going to discard of them in the trash, but instead, she begins to chew on them. Shards of glass slice her gums, tongue and inside of her cheeks as she chews vigorously and swallows. She makes sure to carefully catch the blood with the cloth so it doesn't drip onto the clean floor.

She then scrubs the cheese grater, and as she rinses it, realizes that she somehow shredded her index fingernail on it. She bites the nail at the slice, attempting to remove it. She keeps trying to bite off the pieces of loosened nail but nothing budges. Finally, her teeth rip off the entire nail, down to the exposed meat. She thinks, "This is gonna burn," and puts her hand back into the hot soapy dish water.

She looks out of the kitchen window. Her hands search for dishes in the water. She observes the sky outside darkening and black whirlwinds swirling furiously in the air. Giant manta rays fly in the air like birds. A whirlwind approaches her window and spins into the ground. She can't see it but knows it's drilling into the underground pipes.

The dish water turns murky and black. She feels movement in the water and thinks it's the whirlwind from outside coming up through the drain. But something solid begins to push her hands up out of the water. She examines what arises.

A giant head covered in silver feathers slowly emerges. It stretches from the dark water, revealing the massiveness of its whale-like head. It's evilly arched eyebrows curve over its large, round yellow eyes. Its beak bulges out like a fossil covered sword that ends in a hooked tip.

As it rises, Mercy pulls away and drops back. Her head

slams on the floor and she hears a crack. She lies flat on the floor, watching the man-sized bird step out of the sink. She can't scream because the glass she ate thrashed her vocal chords. The bird and Mercy stare at each other.

It stands straight up, extends its neck, and instantly projects its head at her. It opens its pre-historic looking bill exposing its long, spotted tongue, and lets out a sonic boom sound. She covers her ears in vain because she has already gone deaf from the sound. She watches the bird like a silent movie.

It bends its legs backwards and squats over her, tilting its head to one side. It places one immense three-toed claw on her stomach and holds her down. Its sharp nails tauntingly tap on her chest and perforate the skin over her heart. A powdery flame escapes out of her body with each hole the bird pierces.

Her breath decelerates. She feels warm and calm as her own flames begin to consume her. The water overflows from the sink and starts to fill the house. She knows that this is it for her because the water is steadily turning her heart into ash, and the bird waits to swallow her whole.

Mercy wakes up.

She opens her eyes and looks straight up at the skylight. Her heart flutters, and her skin feels clammy. She feels hot although her body shivers. She wipes her mouth from the drool that dribbled out during the dream. Feeling afraid to move, she lies there immobilized, staring at the ceiling.

A shadow glides over the skylight. At first, Mercy assumes that it is just the trees dancing in the wind outside creating the shadow. The shadow returns, but doesn't move; it just lurks stagnantly over the glass.

Then she notices that it appears in the same shape as the bird from her dream. Two small yellow dots begin to glow brighter in the appropriate places for eyes... and then blink.

She jolts out of bed and rushes to Remedy's room. She turns the light on and climbs under the covers with Remedy.

"Remedy, wake up! Wake up! I'm scared. There was a bird watching me through the skylight."

Remedy covers her eyes from the light. Scrunching her face with frustration, she urges,

"Calm down, and turn off the light! Get in your own bed and go back to sleep."

"I'm not going back in there. Please, just come look really quick. You'll see what I'm talking about."

Mercy pokes at Remedy's shoulder trying to get her to sit up.

Remedy sighs, "Mercy, are you having bad dreams like you always do when you're stressed?"

Mercy childishly nods her head.

"Well, there you go - that's all it is. There's nothing to check out. You're just stressed and imagining things. And birds are probably stuck in your head from that strange owl thing that happened to us."

She presses Mercy's shoulders to lean down onto the pillow, turns off the light on the nightstand, and snuggles under the blanket with her.

"C'mon, you can stay in here with me. I know that's the

only way for either of us to get any sleep tonight."

Mercy tightly holds onto Remedy's arm as they snuggle. After just a few minutes, Remedy's tiny snore echoes in the room. Mercy lies there listening to Remedy's calming breath, and finally begins to feel her own sleep prevailing. As she closes her heavy eyes, feeling herself drift away, she faintly hears the sound of fluttering wings.

All the while, multitudes of large, midnight black ravens perch on the swaying tree branches outside the window, glaring into the moon-lit bedroom. Their unearthly beaks oddly twist upwards. They spread their wings bountifully, as their master flies overhead.

CHAPTER 4

WARNING: TO FLY AWAY

Mercy opens her eyes to the morning sun peeking through the window. She hears the soothing water from the waterfall outside pouring over the rocks, and the faint music of sparrows chirping happily. An empty spot lays next to her in the bed where Remedy should be.

She walks into the living room to find Remedy reading the printed stack of papers from Doc.

"Ugh, Remedy!"

Remedy looks up, a little startled by Mercy's sudden entrance.

"Whoa," Remedy cuts her off, "What the world happened to your face?"

Mercy walks over to the custom designed wall mirror to examine her face. Dried blood marks her mouth and cheek. She notices that there is also dried blood on her hand. She looks closer at her mouth and sees fine cuts inscribed on her lips. She curls her lips open with her fingers to find deeper cuts inside of her mouth.

Her mind flashes back to last night's dream,

"The glass," she mumbles. "I must've bit myself during the nightmare last night. I remember wiping my mouth thinking it was drool, but I guess it was actually blood."

"Ewe," Remedy flares her nostrils and makes an overemphasized frown. Then she excitedly changes the subject,

"Anyhow, go wash up because I want to talk about this amazing info. Where did you get it? I'm so excited that we finally get to know some concrete family history..."

"...Well, I'm glad YOU know. I haven't read anything yet. Those papers were a gift from Doc, and I was saving them to read with you, LATER. And here you are first thing in the morning, just reading your little heart out without me."

Remedy chuckles guiltily, "Ooopsie! I'm sorry. I thought you intentionally left it for me to read."

Mercy just looks at Remedy with her forehead tilted forward and hands on her hips. Remedy grins back like a guilty child who got caught.

"Oh well," Remedy shrugs, "So do you wanna know what the info says or not? It's crazy cool!"

"Might-as-well. Just come in here with me while I jump in the shower because we've gotta be ready before 9 AM."

Mercy showers while Remedy sits on the counter reading aloud from the documents:

Family Name: Kagawi.

Meaning: To Restore.

Location: Region Beyond Kagawa, or "Bird Creek." Exact modern day geographical point unspecified, not mapped on any geological grid. Presumably near a Tibetan region, or near modern-day Bermuda Triangle.

Origin, Blood Line: Kagawi Dynasty.

Closest identifying class: Native American. Specific nationality/ ethnicity/ race unspecified. Appears to be the convergence of early indigenous people: Cushite, Sumerian, Mesopotamian, and modern-day Native American. Discovered artifacts indicative of undetermined extinction. No proof implies extinction by destruction, assimilation or defeat inflicted by another tribe. Very little evidence provides complete background of its tribal origin or of its civilization's lifestyle and beliefs.

The few artifacts found also indicate that this tribe may have had an existence earlier than any recorded genealogical lineage. This small tribe appears to have been of the utmost sacred royal status, deduced by the following deciphered legend:

The small tribe of Kagawi, of the mountainous peaks of Kagawa, who originate from the water in the sky. Guardians turning the sword over the nest of the tree and lighting the cloud. First of the animated dirt, creating all colors of the Creator. Migrating around the double rainbow, fighting the ones disguised in flesh and blood, that attempt to burn down the sacred mountain of all people, the place where the Protector dwells.

Where the rainbow triangle is guarded, and only those can enter who will rebuild life using the power of the complete suit of armor. The large shield quenches the enemy's burning arrows. The belt gives strength to stand strong. Feet covered with peace will heal the broken spirit. The breastplate protects the fire heart.

For the warrior's salvation, put on the helmet and capture the sword of truth to end it all and start again. When the battle begins, the warrior will conquer – the Fire led by Roc in flowing Water. [end]

The Kagawi tribe evidently ascribes victory of an unknown battle to a warrior called "Fire," led by "Roc" (possibly also known as "Flying Thunder"). The warrior will successfully cross over a disorienting triangle, and pass through a double rainbow to gain victory. Since other ancient texts (outside of this tribe) mention this tale and attribute it to the rare Kagawi tribe, it is worthy of valid historical credibility, and not to be considered as a mere myth.

•

•

•

Remedy holds up a piece of paper attached in the documents,

"And there's a picture here, Mer, like an ancient sketch, of two people facing each other standing in mid-air. They both have on the same authentic looking outfits, both with identical long braids on one side and bald on the other side. They're holding body-sized bow and arrows in their hands, and have a string of feathers lining their spines. And stars are flowing down in the background."

Mercy wipes the steam condensation from the glass shower doors to peek through,

"That's so crazy! Wow, it's unbelievable that Doc found that just from a blood sample and a little research. I wish there was more! Hey, did you see the check, too?"

She steps out of the pebbled-floor shower, leaving the water running, and Remedy steps in.

"Oh my goodness, yes, I saw it! Now THAT'S unbelievable! To know that we never have to worry financially ever again!"

Mercy wraps herself in the fresh white towel and re-reads for herself the papers Remedy placed on the sink. She feels compelled to memorize the words of the legend. After a few minutes of etching it into her mind, she glances at her cell phone for the time,

"Uh oh, Rem, we only have about 30 minutes. Hurry up. We'll definitely talk about this later."

"Yeah, definitely. Ok, I'll only be a minute."

Mercy rushes out of the bathroom down the hallway leading to the bedroom. Out of her peripheral vision, she notices a figure of someone in the living room heading swiftly towards her.

She twists around, and realizes it's her own reflection in the living room mirror. She pinches her lips and swallows hard, squeezing the towel knot over her pounding chest. The shower water stops. Mercy doesn't want Remedy to witness her paranoia, so she proceeds to the room.

Remedy and Mercy rush to dress: Mercy slips on black leggings and a long form-fitted red blouse with big black buttons. Remedy fits into a white flowing dress and wraps her waist with a special antique belt. Remedy slides her feet into Roman-style lace-up sandals. Mercy quickly puts on her black stiletto heels, but grabs her sneakers, too. Just in time, they get the call from Dane to come outside to the limousine.

They enter the limo and greet Dane's family, including Jewel. Jewel immediately notices the cuts on Mercy's lips,

"Did you brush your teeth too fast? Because I cut myself all the time when I brush too fast."

Mercy answers smiling, touching her lips with her knuckles, "Oh… no, that wasn't what happened…"

Jewel interjects before Mercy finishes answering, "…Suit yourself!"

Mercy and Remedy look at each other confused, and chuckle discreetly. Dane joins in, too. The family begins to chat among themselves on the car ride to the funeral grounds, so Remedy takes the opportunity to whisper a confession to Mercy,

"Guess what, Mer? I had an interesting dream last

night, too."

"You did? What was yours about?"

"It started with me climbing to the top of an extremely high mountain peak. I had to get to the top because I knew there was a solitary tree up there with what I needed to survive. By the time I pulled myself to the top, a pterodactyl with an exaggerated eagle head came gliding through the air. It had a dragon in its beak and a whale in its claws...

"It landed on the tree, in a giant nest that it made there. And the tree had a sign on it that said 'life.' Then it tossed the dragon up into the air with its massive beak and swallowed it whole. It ripped the whale apart from the blow hole down, and ate it, too. Then I woke up. Isn't it weird how we both had crazy dreams?"

"Yeah it is! Your dream seems like it has some crazy subliminal meaning. I've gotta tell you my dream later. It's *still* freaking me out."

They look at each other with raised eyebrows, holding hands. Seeing the fear in Mercy's eyes, Remedy says,

"Don't worry, Mer. They were just dreams." She squeezes Mercy's hand and smiles. Then observes Mercy's eyes move up to look behind her out of the window. Remedy turns around to see what has caught Mercy's attention.

Legions of tall, ugly birds line the side of the road croaking and hissing, intensely watching the mass of funeral cars roll by. Most are huge in stature, over five feet tall, with ox-like body shapes. Very ghastly by sight.

Fleshy featherless pink heads textured with gray peeling scales, completely black eyes, and blood-stained bills. They all stand transfixed, spreading their wings to expose their threateningly extensive wingspan.

Since Dane has been inconspicuously admiring Mercy the whole time, he also looks in the direction that she does. Astounded at the invasion, he asks aloud for anyone to answer,

"Is it normal that random birds are crowding around like this?"

Mercy and Remedy remark at the same time, "Wow, very Alfred Hitchcock-esque."

Uncle Les and Jewel look out the window.

Jewel taps on the window,

"Well hello my fine feathered friends!"

Uncle Les affirms,

"Oh yes, it's normal. The big ones look like marabou storks. Granted, *these* are a little bigger, and more ferocious in appearance, but surely belong to that family. And I never knew they could fly backwards, like that one," he points out.

One of the human-sized birds is contorting its

wings strangely to fly backwards, although its head remains forward-facing. It flies low and slow, nearer and nearer to the car, hissing and gurgling. Then it swiftly rolls over the roof out of sight.

"Where'd it go?" Mercy and Remedy yell out.

Everyone searches outside the windows to see if the

giant creature flew away. But they cannot see any trace of it in the sky or on the ground.

Jewel adds,

"Those marabou storks are known for stalking funerals, the little critters – well, BIG little critters, I should say. But they never do anything like that – how odd! He's probably just very hungry and, therefore, losing his sense of direction. When I was young, my grandfather lost his sense of direction one time, while we were driving. We ended up in a cemetery. To make a long story short, he explained that we needed to get out and dance on the graves. And that's the *first* time I danced on a grave."

Everyone stays quiet, not knowing which part of any of that to respond to.

The funeral party drives into the forest area where the outside ceremony is set up beautifully. Hundreds of people park their cars and walk to the designated seating area which faces the stage. Mercy, Dane and Remedy walk together towards the family section in the front. All the guests take their seats as well.

Mercy nibbles on her painted fingernails, silently practicing the speech on the index card in her lap. Dane detects her anxiety,

"You'll do fine, Mer. No worries."

Mercy raises her eyebrows and reciprocates a smile at Dane. When she glances up at Dane, she sees Dane's ex-girlfriend, Echo, approaching them in the background. She hastily puts her head back down as if she doesn't see Echo walking over.

Echo's short hair, dyed variations of faded green, bounces in the breeze. Her bangs swoop from one side across her forehead to the other side of her face. Her eyes are lined heavily with black eyeshadow, creating a cat-eye effect. The combination of the hair color and make-up accentuates her violet-colored eyes.

Mercy always thought Echo was intimidatingly striking, but Remedy disagrees. Remedy thinks Echo's internal ugliness seeps through and overshadows any external appeal.

"Hi, Dane," Echo says in a sultry voice. "I'm so sorry for your loss. Lewis was a great man, and will be missed immensely." She places her petite fingers on his muscular shoulder.

Dane responds solemnly, "Thanks."

Echo stands there staring at him as if expecting something.

"Well, can I have a hug?" she sweetly says, holding her arms out from her lusty body.

Dane scrunches his eyebrows, then unintentionally glances at Mercy, who still has her head down nervously focused on the script. Echo is not pleased by his reaction,

"Oh because *she's* here? Ok... it's ok... Don't worry about it, Daney-boy. I'm sure we'll get to spend some alone time together, once she's gone. I will *console* you then."

She strokes his neck tenderly as she pulls her arms back to her sides. She looks at Mercy,

"Hi... um, Kasey, right?!"

Mercy doesn't respond, unaware that Echo purposely

and provokingly called her by the wrong name. In a more condescending tone, Echo repeats,

"Hello – KASEY?!"

Remedy quickly jumps in, "Her name is **not** Kasey. It's Mercy: M-E-R-C-Y!"

Dane and Mercy both look at Remedy in shock. Remedy continues,

"C'mon, Echo. Don't act like you don't know her name. She's been Dane's best friend since before he even knew you existed. But maybe that's one of the many reasons why Dane broke up with you: because you have an unjustifiably rude attitude."

Remedy rolls her eyes, "Just give it up, and go worry about dying your hair to look like moldy cotton candy." She shakes her head at Echo, then turns the opposite way.

Echo stands shocked at Remedy's unexpected jabs. But Mercy and Dane aren't surprised. They know that Remedy will break her tranquil disposition in a heartbeat to protect her sister.

Dane smiles up at Echo,

"Maybe you should take your seat now. I see my Uncle Les heading up on the platform to start."

Embarrassed, Echo simply nods her head, realizing that she has no place there with Dane and the girls. She walks away briskly. Mercy and Dane bust out laughing, and nudge Remedy, who has regained her cool composure.

"What?!" Remedy rhetorically questions as they nudge her, knowing she wants to laugh, too.

Uncle Les walks on stage and gets the crowd's attention by speaking into the microphone. He starts the memorial by first reading the obituary, followed by the eulogy he wrote. Afterward, he announces that there is a special note that Lewis wanted highlighted at his funeral. He invites up Jewel to give the special comments.

"This may be quite uncomfortable for some to hear," Jewel says to the audience in a serious tone. "I didn't get to skim over this note until just before I came up on stage, and I was puzzled as to why he would request this be publicly announced..."

She wipes her mouth with a handkerchief and sips water from the glass on the podium.

"But Lewis died in what some would consider the most disgraceful way a man could die... **penis- less**. How this happened? We don't know. But he wanted others to remember that the physical things in life aren't the driving force of happiness. Physical things don't provide lasting satisfaction."

An attendant scurries to the stage with a folded note as Jewel keeps talking. She opens the note but merely glances at it before she continues,

"...Everyone who knew Lewis, wouldn't have even guessed he was in this situation because he was so generous with what he *did* possess and what he was able to do. His wife can attest to that!..."

She winks at the mourning and bewildered widow, Connie, in the front row sitting next to Dane. Dane forcefully shakes his head and does a scissor motion with his fingers at Jewel. Jewel notices but is confused by it, so keeps going.

"…Despite being **penis-less**, he walked with integrity, not focused on the negativity that comes with such a burden…"

Another attendant runs to the stage frantically with a big piece of paper and thick, black writing on it, and holds it practically in front of Jewel's face. She finally reads the note and acknowledges the attendant,

"Oh my – oh my word! Thank you for that note."

Then she returns to addressing the audience,

"Everyone, I apologize for my reading errors and misspoken words! Lewis was PENNILESS when he died, **not** … um … *penis*-less. He was penniless – out of money. Yeah, that's a lot less embarrassing. Now it all makes sense."

Most guests cover their mouths or keep their heads down, while others can't hold in their snickering. Flustered and ready to get Jewel off the stage, Les takes over the mic again and gently pushes her to exit the stage. He proceeds with calling for the burial of the ashes, forgetting to call Mercy up to read her speech. Mercy quickly shoves the speech into her purse feeling relieved that she doesn't have to speak after all.

Dane leans over to her, his lips lightly touching her ear as he whispers, "Don't think you're getting off that easily. I still want to hear what you wrote."

She playfully rolls her eyes at him. He pinches her knee, making her squirm and giggle. She feels another tickle on the opposite side of her neck and flinches, thinking it's a spider. She swats at the furry movement crawling on her skin. A feather falls from her shoulder to her lap. Relieved, she realizes it was a feather, not a bug.

Without warning, an insanely loud croaking noise disrupts the funeral's awkward moment. Everyone looks around for the source of the disturbance. Again, a terrifying solitary screech roars out into the air. A series of gurgling caws ensue like a diabolical orchestra. Then colonies of tall, massive bodies press through the tree vines that hang like falling rope.

CHAPTER 5

WARNING: INTO THE DARK

The horde of marabou storks methodically steps out

from the thick forest trees, encircling the crowd. Their talons crush dried leaves as they walk out like determined undertakers. They bellow throatily to summon others.

Instantly, dozens of vultures appear like a flash-storm of feathered hail. They hop down from the highest branches above, thumping to the ground with confident aggression, screaming from their hooked bills. Heads and chests full of disarranged brown feathers accenting their strong wing bones, which resemble men's muscled arms. Their bright red eyes glare at the humans. They begin to bob their burly bodies like fighters do when waiting for the start bell in a ring.

Mercy grabs Remedy and Dane's hands, "What the --! Something is wrong. The catering truck is over there. Why are they coming over here after us, and not the food?"

"More importantly," Remedy adds, "Do they think **we are** the food?"

The storks crouch down in raptor position, and turn their heads left to right at each other. Their long blood-stained bills clatter powerfully in communication, resembling the sound of wooden baseball bats slamming together.

Nobody moves but everyone looks on with terror in their eyes, sensing looming danger. As the birds creep in closer on the crowd, people begin to whimper and yell out at the birds. Someone warns, "We're completely out-numbered!" Another screams out, "Start throwing stuff at 'em!" And another, "Punch them!"

The storks stop clattering, and the vultures stop bobbing. All their psychotic, blank eyes fixate on the humans. It becomes a staring contest, in which everyone's gaze remains as motionless as a devastated wasteland. Everyone keeps still and silent, until a sonic boom flares from the sky.

The people instinctively cover their ears and look up. In that instant, the birds turn invisible. Altogether transfigured into an invisible mob, they ambush the crowd. They lash out with invisible ruthlessness on the unsuspecting humans.

People try to scramble, only to get caught by the unseen monster birds' natural weapons. Dane and the girls drop to the ground and sneak to the center of the crowd. Chaotic sounds of flapping, growling, ripping flesh, and screaming take over.

The birds skillfully pierce and slice at the skin over the hearts of the people and slurp out their veins like wet noodles. Not wasting a single drop of blood, they drain the humans of all life. With every calculated strike, the bodies collapse.

Mercy and Remedy scream watching the people trapped by the invisible strength that pounces them. Their bodies drained by extraordinary might, crushing their bones to peck out the osseous matter. The manslayers carefully squeeze each person's head against the gravel until their skull pops open. Then they scratch through the cortex. They gobble up specific pieces of each person's brain.

Once they've accomplished each attack, they reappear for a blurry moment. The storks' drooping nodules on their long, wrinkled necks engorge with the insides of the humans they consume. The vultures cock their heads up and down to swallow down their prey. Then they at once disappear again for their next unperceivable assault.

Just as Dane, Mercy and Remedy figure out that the birds are closing in on them, Mercy spots an opening in the forest a few feet away. She removes her stiletto heels.

"We've gotta run – NOW!" Mercy yells out to Dane and Remedy.

Mercy leads the dash through the commotion. They try not to trample the victims that have already passed into the dark death of the birds. They feel scared, sad, and angry hurdling over the fallen, but don't stop or look back.

Miraculously, they safely slip into the entrance of the forest and find two giant boulders edged under a decaying trunk, covering a strip of flowing river. They crawl into the water and in-between the rocks, taking refuge there from the unwarranted savagery.

In a petrified whisper, Mercy asks, "Are you kidding? These deadly things turn *invisible*? How are we supposed to escape from something invisible? This isn't a fair fight."

A moment later, a mortified young child bravely ventures towards their location. Before they can jump out to help the child take cover with them, a vulture appears like a gruesome giant in comparison to the small kid. The scene happens in slow motion:

The child looks back helplessly at the beast, and faint from fear, falls to the dirt. Folded face down in a fetal position, crying and screaming for help, the vulture unyieldingly advances nearer. The three jolt out from their temporary haven towards the bird with every endeavor to save the precious youngster.

Their sudden movement, though, stuns the vulture causing it to vomit out a jellied, gaseous substance. The gooey vomit covers the toddler and creates a cloud of gaseous smoke that blocks their view and stops them from their rescue attempt. They cough and wave at the air trying to clear the toxic cloud. Meanwhile, the sound of the child's cry is abruptly cut off and replaced by a sound of flesh ripping.

After the storm of belligerently fluttering wings stops, the air grows still and eerily quiet.

The cloud of gas clears, exposing the child's lifeless corpse in front of them. It rests hollow on the gravel; like all the other corpses they are now able to see. All of them, cold and pale, the result of the birds' vicious embalming attack. Just mere remains of flattened outer shells of pale skin without brains, blood or muscle density, which were sucked out of them.

Dane drops to his knees at the sight of the massacre, realizing his *whole* family is gone now.

Mercy cries and trembles, outraged at the injustice, "Only a baby! An innocent baby." She covers her mouth, "Why? Why is this happening?"

"Because they're animals ... wild animals gathered for their feast. It's what they do," Remedy mutters, the tears flooding her eyes.

"Not like this," Dane forces himself to stand up. "Like

Mercy said before, something is wrong."

Mercy peers into the sky at nothing, "I can feel that they're gone ... I wonder where they went."

Dane bitterly says through his teeth, "Probably off to their next killing frenzy," rubbing both hands up his face and through the curls on his head.

"Or maybe," Remedy adds, "They're still here, just waiting."

Remedy grabs Mercy's hand, giving her an accidental static-shock, as usual. They squeeze their tangled grip, looking at one another with glassy eyes. She and Mercy simultaneously look at Dane and ask,

"What do we do now?"

He pauses briefly to think, then urges,

"We get in the limo - the keys are usually left in the ignition. And we drive the heck outta here!"

He scouts out the car,

"Look! There it is." He points out for the girls to locate

it, too. "Try to stay together. Let's break for it as fast as we can on the count of three. One – Two – Three!"

They dart through the sprouting flowers and hollow bloodless corpses. They leap over those slain, including Echo, Uncle Les, Connie and Jewel. Crying as they run, partly for those eliminated and partly for fear of their own lives. Dane takes the lead with Mercy close behind. Not as athletically swift, however, Remedy trails back. Mercy and Dane don't realize this, though, until they reach the limo.

Dane jumps into the driver's seat and finds the keys in the ignition just as he thought. He attempts to start the engine. Mercy sees Remedy in the distance and shouts out frantically,

"C'MON, REM!" She flinches to run back towards Remedy, but Dane reaches out through the open car door and grabs her arm. He sternly orders,

"Stay here!"

She quickly redirects her attention back to Remedy, seeing a descending shadow eclipse Remedy's racing body. Mercy yells out,

"Hurry up! C'mon, RUN Remedy!"

She reaches out for Remedy, grabs her hand and pulls her to the car.

The shadow warps over the car after they jump in and close the doors. They hear a menacing low toned caw pass along with the shadow, feeling its vibration like a bass guitar strum in amplified speakers. Dane continues to attempt the clicking engine, while Mercy and Remedy hug. Breathing heavily, they repeat "I love you" to each other.

"It's gonna be ok. I'm here. It's gonna be ok," Remedy tells Mercy, but is actually telling herself. "It's gonna be ok. We're gonna get outta here soon. It's all gonna be fine."

Mercy growls, "Ugh! Why is this happening? I can't even take one more second of this unexplained attack! It's not gonna be ok ... They've already killed people, and they're not gonna stop!"

Mercy's anger boils up inside. Everything she has ever felt in life, the pain, the sadness, the urge to run, is all coming to a head now. Feeling trapped, vulnerable, scared, helpless and most of all angry, she knows she must either fight or just give up.

Then in an instant, a thought flashes in her mind, and she asks,

"Wait a minute, what if we try the Kagawa legend? It mentioned *flowing water*. I think we should try to get back to the river and follow the water! That's where we were safe during the attack, hiding between the rocks in the water. The water is *the shield* that quenches the burning arrows."

Dane looks back, "Well, might-as-well give it a shot because this hunk of junk isn't starting for some reason. Those flying demons might have dismantled all the cars."

Mercy looks at Remedy for her approval of the water plan, too. Remedy contemplates for a moment, then gives a half grin,

"I have faith in you, sis. Let's do it."

Remedy converts her long white dress into shorts by tucking the bottom hemline into her belt and fastens it in place. Mercy braids her hair in two long French-braids, and tightens the laces on her sneakers that she thankfully brought with her and left in the limo. Dane straps on the emergency backpack from the door compartment, which includes water, antihistamines, antiseptics, a flashlight, a couple cans of fruit, and some chocolate protein bars.

In a close huddle, they cautiously walk out looking up into the sky for any sign of the monsters. They make it safely into the wilderness, passing the boulders where they previously hid, and follow the stream of cold, sparkling water. The minutes seamlessly stretch into hours.

They delve deep into the woods. Their eyes feast on the ostentatious tree trunks that sprout like arms from the ground. Branches like gnarled fingers tug at their clothes while they go by. After a couple hours, dusk insatiably sets in, devouring the sunlight from the already dim forest trajectory.

Dane gets the flashlight from the backpack, but doesn't turn it on yet to save battery. Mercy pulls her glasses from her purse and puts them on. Remedy pulls her long hair up into a high bun and secures it with the hair tie on her wrist.

They all notice the water stream dwindling down to a narrow stagnation of connecting puddles. But the sound of gushing water in the near distance catches their attention, giving them hope of security. They believe that the more water, the better chances of survival.

"Sounds like a waterfall up ahead," Remedy exclaims.

An opening through the trees reveals a large flat mountain peak, covered with an unexplainable amount of flora and fauna species like they've never seen before. Leaving the forest enclosure, they enter the middle of the open square terrain that ends in a rapidly rolling waterfall. The water sounds like glass breaking endlessly, and the cold drops splattering on them feel just the same.

They analyze their surroundings. An unusual sky colored a shade of neon pink, filled with golden clouds, creates a most surreal feeling. The granite cliff displays giant trees like a sacred garden of the gods, steeped in mist and drenched in the facade of serenity. The enormity of the view brings the reality of their small existence.

"Whelp," Mercy yells out over the crashing water, "the water has led us here. Should we jump or turn back into the forest?"

Before they can answer, an invisible force of gravity pulls all of them into the plummeting water. The turbulent current tackles them down. Mercy struggles to keep her senses, floundering around like a fish. She gulps down foam that sprays at her.

Finally, the rapid flow of liquid hydrogen and oxygen effortlessly drops her into the calm, wet darkness below.

Mercy feels her body dip into a pool of warm water. Bubbles blanket her body. She paddles up rigorously for air, lifting her head over the surface once she reaches the top.

She looks around for Dane and Remedy, but because her glasses disappeared during the fall, everything looks dark and fuzzy. She hears a cough nearby, and makes out Dane's image crawling up onto a rock. She swims in his direction.

He pulls her up as she arrives to the rock. They embrace, shivering and exhausted.

"Can you see Rem anywhere?" she asks, looking out into the water.

Still holding firm to the flashlight, Dane replies, "Good thing I have a strong grip, and good thing this is waterproof."

He flashes the light over the translucent water in hopes of seeing Remedy. Nothing appears in sight. Then they hear a fatigued voice from a few hundred feet away, near the waterfall drop. Dane flashes the light in that direction, switching to the high beam mode on the handle.

Remedy dangles by her belt from a sturdy branch, caught in the backlash of the waterfall. Mercy and Dane notice her erratically wailing her arms and legs. They begin yelling out her name until she recognizes them.

"Stop wiggling," Mercy demands, "And unlatch your belt!"

Dane shouts out, "Unlatch your belt! Let yourself drop, Remy!"

Remedy scrambles to unlatch her belt. Her body wiggles, then finally slides out of the entrapment. She begins to fall. Mercy suddenly feels nauseous; a feeling like something bad is about to happen. She feels the voracious presence of the gluttonous creatures waiting to capture her twin as their prey.

Before Remedy hits the water below, the goliath white owl stealthily swoops down from nowhere and steals her body in mid-air. They hear the delicate bones in Remedy's body snap in the owl's clutch as it glides up into the dark clouds with her. The owl vanishes, without a single flap.

Mercy feels her body begin to quiver violently. She feels like her heart could literally stop beating right then and there, and that her whole existence will fall apart. She stares hopelessly into the night sky, unable to speak, waiting for Remedy to somehow reappear. Shock possesses her.

"Mercy?" Dane wraps his arms around her tense shoulders from behind. But she doesn't feel him because she's numb.

"Mercy?"

Silence. She doesn't react to his voice or his touch. She can't.

"We've gotta get outta here, Mer. They're watching us."

"I don't care... anymore."

Something moves in the water in front of them. Dane flashes the light there, and they see a manta ray float to the surface with one of the owl's molted feathers and Remedy's belt attached to it. Dane picks the belt out of the water and hands it to Mercy.

Her shoulders start twitching as she begins to dissolve in tears. She can't catch her breath, "Rem – was – all – I – had. My – everything. My – rock. I – can't – breathe."

She grabs her chest over her heart. Her fingernails rip holes in her blouse and dig into her skin. Dane restrains her hand and presses it on his cheek to redirect her emotion. She feels his wet skin, which helps snap her out of hyperventilating.

"I'm sorry, Mer. Remy was my sister, too. We have to keep going, though."

He moves her stoic body to the rocky trail bordering the water. As he adjusts his soggy backpack, Mercy's eyes scroll up to a tree. She makes out a blurry shadow among the branches.

She can't take her eyes away from its whale-like skull shaking wildly side to side. She hears a cringe-worthy moo sound from its fossilized snapping bill, and perceives that it is the bird from her nightmare. Its supernatural carcass sits on top of the tree, the branches somehow undisturbed as if the giant was weightless.

She locks her stare on it for what feels to her like an eternity. She knows it stares back at her although her vision isn't clear. She imagines its sneering bill and deranged round eyes mocking her. Then she sees it arch its back, dropping its head lower as it rounds into a hunchback. Three sets of wings flare out from behind it.

Dane notices her staring up at the tree, so he flashes the light there,

"What is it, Mer?"

But instantly, it disappears, blending into the star-studded backdrop. Mercy wipes her tear stained cheeks and in a somber tone responds,

"Nothing. It was nothing. Let's just keep going."

She tries to sound brave, wrapping Remedy's belt around her head and shoving the feather in the side,

"When love is ripped away, all that's left is war."

They continue without speaking in the muddy soil alongside the still river in the dark. Dane travels in front of Mercy, shining the flashlight a couple feet ahead to watch their path. He occasionally shines it up into the air to watch for the predators. Their feet sink into the mushy soil with each step. Mud squishes around their shoes.

Dane and Mercy both stay quiet as they hike further. Dane knows Mercy's mind is filled with the reality of

Remedy's absence, and that alone is too much noise for her to be able to talk with him. He hesitates to break the silence, but compassionately says,

"I'm here for you, and we'll get through this. Don't worry, ok?"

She doesn't answer.

"K, Mer?"

No answer.

He stops walking and looks back. Mercy is no longer directly behind him.

"MER?!"

He frantically flashes the light all around. He hears a muffled sound from the mud a few steps back and sees red hair shooting out from the wet gravel. He returns to the area, and holds the flashlight handle in his mouth so he can excavate the soil from around Mercy's submerged body.

Bubbles trickle up from the mud, and he sees her fingertips wiggle. He impulsively extracts her hand, then feels down her arm to her bent elbow. He forcefully pulls her up with a strong grip. She rises, hysterically digging her way out with his help.

She spits out mud and blows it out of her nose. She hurriedly grabs at her feet and frantically unlaces her shoes. Dane helps her as she kicks them off, moaning and scratching at her feet. Dane shines the light on her limbs.

Bright red fire ants the size of hamsters, scuttle all over her swollen feet and legs. They scramble out from her sneakers. Elongated antennae on their alien looking heads bend repeatedly in the air like snake tongues. Their pinching mandibles make hungry clamping noises, and their hairy abdomens release a foul-smelling odor.

Mercy cries, "They pulled me into their hole by my feet and started biting me! I can't feel my legs!"

Dane beats off the meaty ants with the flashlight, and lifts Mercy up completely off the ground into his arms. She tightly wraps her arms around his neck. He kicks the ants like soccer balls out of his way when they attempt to retrieve Mercy again. He starts running as fast as humanly possible despite the mud's attempt to gobble him down.

He has no idea where he's going and can barely see with the flashlight jiggling around while he runs. He hears Mercy's dazed voice begging for a safe hiding place to rest. Just then, thunder quakes and lightning flashes over a cave in the distance. He decides to run towards the cave with guidance from the natural elements.

The trees open like umbrellas behind them, blocking the view of the path they leave behind. Invisible wings of the predators camouflage themselves in the sound of each umbrella tree popping open.

Dane continues towards the dancing light, carrying his Mercy all the way. Sharp rocks and branches leave small but nasty lacerations all over Dane's body as he runs through the dark. He feels a lurking presence all around him, but doesn't stop to look. Finally, they reach the cave.

The cave's entrance looks like two facial profiles getting ready to perform a forbidden kiss. Its serene majesty draws Dane inside.

Prismatic purple, orange and blue lights bounce off the metallic marble rocks. They bounce onto the pristine water, and from the water back to the rocks. This mirror-like behavior allows for the exhibition of stalactites hanging like stone icicles from the roof. Their stalagmite counterparts loom up from the ground under them like jagged crystallized gems.

Pools within pools of idle water flood the entire floor of the deep cavern. Clear froth gently mists over the still liquid surface, giving off a peculiarly sweet scent. Dane finds a patch of dry earth to lie Mercy down carefully. He gives her an antihistamine to swallow for the pain, and treats her wounds with antiseptic patches.

"Thank you," she humbly says.

"My pleasure, Mer," he remarks, focused on dabbing the bites with medicine. "How do you feel?"

"I'm less dizzy now. And I can feel my legs again, although they're burning and itching like crazy!"

He delicately pushes infected puss out from the bites with alcohol pads. He catches a whiff of the same pungent smell that the fire ants released. Open holes remain where the stinky puss dribbles out from.

"We should get you washed up, Mer. Who knows what this stuff is."

"And then we can eat something?" she asks.

He laughs because only Mercy would think about food at a time like this. "Yea, then we can crack open the fruit and protein bars. Can you walk now?"

"Yea," she stands up and begins to undress.

He turns away respectfully, although extremely tempted to look, and starts scraping the mud off the clothes she drops. She quickly dips herself in the warm water and wipes her arms, face and legs.

"Here you go,"

He takes out a few napkins for her to dab dry with, and leaves the clothes next to her, still forcing himself to not look. She puts her clothes back on quickly and sits next to him.

"Yikes," she says looking at Dane's minor injuries, "Are

you alright?"

He analyzes his wounds, "Ah, this is nothing compared to what *you* went through. I'm alright."

She looks up at the only dark patch of the roof, "This is the weirdest day of my life!" she says while simultaneously thinking, 'I wish Remedy was here.'

"You're telling me," he opens the cans of fruit from the backpack.

He hands her one can and he takes the other. They eat together in silence. Loud thunder cracks the air outside of the cave. Mercy looks out near the entrance for rain,

"That's weird. I thought thunder only happens when it rains."

They shrug it off and go on eating. Thunder and lightning continue to crash from the heavens without any accompanying rainfall. All the while, unbeknownst to Mercy and Dane, the featherless one in the dark crevices above watches them. Rapidly changing its lenses, moving its third transparent membrane to

112

zoom in on Dane's face. It sneakily waits to make its move.

[CHAPTER 6]

WARNING: OF A FIRE KISS

"So, what do you think – do you think we're safe here until daylight?" Dane asks Mercy when they're finished eating.

"Honestly, I don't know what's safe anymore, Dane. Location and time seem to be no factor for these creatures in bird's clothing. I just don't know. I can usually come up with some grand optimistic view of things ... but I honestly see no way out of this one. I just want to keep running. Run away and never stop!"

Mercy dips her hand in the hole that's next to her, which looks like a bowl of yellow daisies. When she does, a rush of golden butterflies flutter up, sounding like lips smacking. They fly away and blend into the bouncing lights. Mercy watches how freely they escape.

Dane silently looks out into the dark depths of the cave. A runaway breeze whistles through the smooth metallic rocks of marble which are lined with yellow stripes from rusted water calcium. Silver moonbeams sneak in through a small hole in the roof above them.

"Remember that rock band named, *Switchfoot?*"

Mercy looks at Dane awkwardly, trying to figure out why he'd ask that question in a time like this,

"Y-e-s. What about them?"

"I just thought," he interrupts himself with a chuckle, causing his dimples to crease into his chiseled cheeks. Then he continues,

"I just thought about one of their songs – that one called, 'Meant To Live.' How it says, '*We were meant to live for so much more. Have we lost ourselves? Somewhere, we **are** inside.*' Those words are so deep … just thought it matches this moment."

"Uh huh, ok. I think I see where you're going with that connection. Like: we're feeling lost, but we're actually inside … of a cave."

"Ok," Dane nods his head, although that's not at all

what he meant, "Close enough."

"I guess that wasn't the right answer," she says scrunching her nose. "I can't think right now. You know I'm a deep thinker normally. I'm just not in the mood right now."

He laughs again.

"What? What's so funny?"

"Eh, it's ok. You don't need to know."

"Yes, I do, Dane. Tell me why you're over there analyzing random deep lyrics in your head, and yet you're cracking up at the same time."

He rubs his eyes and laughs, "No, Mer. It's ok. Forget it."

Knowing he's ticklish, Mercy jams her fingers in his sides and starts wiggling her fingers roughly,

"Tell me why you're laughing or I'm not going to stop tickling you."

"Ouch! Is that your idea of tickling?" Dane restrains

her. "You're going to kill me, jabbing those nails into my sides. Who taught you how to tickle?"

"Hush up! I'm the best tickler, ever." She twists out of his grip and pinches his neck, "Just tell me why you were laughing, punk. You're laughing at **me**, aren't you?"

"Well … not at *you*. More like, at the *situation*. I just think it's funny that the band called 'Switch*foot*' pops in my head right after your feet are attacked by unearthly little critters. Get it, the irony?"

Mercy shakes her head,

"Yea, I got cha' fella. Your little play on words there to mock my suffering feet after getting attacked by alien ants. Not awkward or nerdy at all. Totally hilarious."

He gently squeezes her knee,

"It really is, though, when you think about it. We have no idea what's going on, where we even are or what creatures will reveal themselves next. And the first thing that I think of is a *Switchfoot* song because my mind is focused on feet, of all things. That's not funny to you?"

Mercy just looks at him, resting her cheek on her fist, chin on her palm, with her elbow posted on her knee. She yawns obnoxiously,

"The things that amuse you, surprise me. If I could only see into that mind of yours, Dane."

He pauses, and smiles,

"If you could see into my mind, it'd be like you're looking in a mirror ... because you're pretty much all that's on my mind, all the time."

Pleasantly surprised by his words, she smiles and shakes her head. He scoots closer next to her so that their bodies touch. Their gentle collision sparks romantic tension.

"There's that smile I love to see," he seductively caresses her jawline. His fingers drift up her smiling cheek, and back down over her bottom lip to her chin.

"You're so silly, Dane," she says, hoping to divert the feeling of pulsating attraction.

"Oh yeah?" he replies flirtatiously, blocking her attempted aversion, and creating an even more palpable magnetism.

"Yeah ..." she bashfully looks down feeling her ears turn hot, knowing her whole face is probably tomato red by now.

"Mer, I know this might not be the right time, and it will probably make this moment even more awkward if you don't feel the same, but I just have to tell you that I really love you. More than a guy should love someone who isn't even his girl."

She smiles, trying to ignore the itchy sensation coming from the unattractive bites on her feet. She jokes for him to continue, but is serious, wanting to drown in his expressions towards her.

As he speaks, she listens, removing Remedy's belt and owl feather from her head.

"I love that you can see people for who they truly are, and love them anyway. You aren't naïve to the devil in people, yet you choose to see the God in them. And you treat people unbiasedly, as if you're certain that nobody is completely defined by either their devilish side *or* their godly side. You love people for all they are."

"I love *you* for all that you are, you mean?" she says while un-braiding her damp red hair so that it alluringly drapes around her shoulders.

She looks irresistible to him while combing her hair with her fingertips. He can't resist anymore. He goes in for a kiss, sweetly stamping his perfect lips onto hers. As soon as their lips touch, they both feel a quantum portal open around them, suspending time and fusing their souls together.

They connect passionately and unrelentingly, not holding back an ounce of love expressed through the kiss. Dane melts in the heat of her soft, succulent affection, and Mercy clings to his every move becoming one with his being.

She feels their mutual magnetic pull. She soaks in the feeling of blissful surrender. He opens his eyes, seeing Mercy still with closed eyes in a romantic trance. She feels him looking at her and opens her eyes, too. When she does,

Dane pulls away.

"What's wrong, Dane?"

He pauses, then answers, "Look at your reflection in the water."

She bends over the water, dumbfounded by what she sees. Her eyes are entirely blood red, with no trace of white sclera around the iris or black pupil in the center. She blinks her eyes in the reflection to see if they'll change back to what she's always known as normal, but they don't change.

Then she looks at Dane, "What's going on?"

Lightning strikes and thunder follows. Mercy hears Remedy's voice in the thunder say,

"You are the Fire, the warrior that consumes completely in the final phase. I am your Roc, the Flying Thunder, the power that gives you endurance. Keep going. Finish your mission."

Mercy yells out to the sky, "What mission?"

Perplexed at Mercy's sudden outburst into the air with

her palms up towards the sky, Dane asks,

"Are you okay, Mer?"

He touches her shoulder. His fingertips graze over something hard and lumpy protruding from the skin over her heart. She feels it, too.

She rises to her feet and pulls down her shirt. She uncovers a square breastplate made of cylinder bones welded securely into her chest. They both gasp.

The cylinder bones contain etched cryptic symbols that resemble groups of stars. The breastplate is backed by a translucent sheet of beautiful burnt-orange sardius stone. Her beating heart pounds beneath the translucent sheet of sardius like a raging furnace trying to break free. Speckled red and yellow jasper stones seal each corner of the breastplate. The infused gemstones sparkle against the four singed edges of the breastplate.

"That's ... so ... awesome!" Dane remarks with his hand over his mouth, leaving only his bright, copper-colored eyes exposed. "Can I touch it?"

He grazes his palm over the naturally formed breastplate.

"You're amazing, Mer! It's beautiful. Does it hurt?"

"No. No, it doesn't. It actually feels like ... like it's always been there, although I know it hasn't ... Or at least I've never noticed. I can't explain it."

He leans down and tenderly kisses her breastplate. Her intense heat causes his lips to chap into smoldered rock. Steam puffs out of him instead of breath, and he suddenly feels faint. Sweating profusely, he stumbles from instantaneous heat stroke, but Mercy supports him.

"Whoa, Dane! It's okay, I got you."

As she helps him lie down on the ground, she hears a vaguely familiar shrilling voice ring out from the dark ceiling,

"No, you don't have him. *WE* do."

She looks up, studiously combing through the stalactites to find the face that matches the voice. An obnoxious laugh cackles out from the dark crevices above. Mercy recognizes the tone of the laugh but cannot match a face to the voice. She hears it screech,

"Now can I take you, Mercy?" Its tone dips to a deep, sinister one, "Let – me – take – you!"

She flinches, and keeps looking around the cave. Noticing her progressive paranoia, Dane asks,

"Are you ok, Mer?"

She looks at him confused,

"Didn't you hear that voice? First, the voice in the thunder that sounded like Rem. Now a familiar voice from the roof in here. You didn't hear either of them?"

Dane shakes his head, concerned that the trauma of this entire situation is triggering Mercy to hear things that don't exist. Mercy continues trying to explain herself,

"I heard a voice say, 'Let me'... wait a minute, I know that voice. It's the stranger in the park!"

"Who? Which park?"

"I don't have time to explain."

The annoying voice mimics her, "I don't have time to explain."

Dane looks blankly at her with sweat running over his puppy dog eyelids. She realizes she must sound crazy, and pretends to drop the subject,

"Never mind. Just rest. We both need rest. Close your eyes."

He pauses. His eyes drill into hers with worried scrutiny. He motions for her to come towards his lips, then gives her another arresting kiss more passionate than their first. Despite his charcoaled lips, his kiss feels soft and sweet to her. When they separate, he whispers in her ear,

"It'll all be ok."

He smiles his beautiful smile and pecks her nose.

"Close your eyes, and rest, Dane."

She leans her back against the wall, and presses his clammy head onto her lap. After he gets comfortable, she sprinkles water onto his flushed cheeks. She leans over and kisses his closed eyelids. He smiles. She kisses his neck, noticing his rising temperature.

"I always knew you were too hot for me, Mer," he whispers.

"Whatever," she grins, "Go to sleep."

He grins back, then instantly knocks out.

She uses the time to examine the lid of the cave again for the owner of the mysterious voice. From the corner of her vision, she spots a slippery shadow sliding upside down over the jagged surface. A beam of refracted light reveals an appalling cocoon hanging, wrapped in a black coat of leather.

The uncanny leather cocoon smoothly flares out with the elegance of a flower opening. Its featherless pinions stretch out, making a crinkling noise like unfolding paper. A furry head contorts from the leather draping, rotating to face her. With wide eyes and a joker's stoic grin, it imposes a lunatic stare at Mercy. Its open mouth shows a string of dry veins caught in its sharp teeth.

It speaks without moving its mouth or using words, but Mercy hears and understands its voice,

"The journey doesn't end where you suspect."

Mercy asks,

"How do you know what I suspect?"

The creature slants its head and answers,

"You suspect we're trying to kill you."

"Well, aren't you?"

The creature laughs rambunctiously,

"We're only doing what we have been ordered to do."

Mercy squints her red eyes in disgust that some cretin would order the assassination of innocent people, including Remedy. She seethes,

"Ordered by who?"

It screeches, "By YOU!" and points at her with the sharp nail on the middle joint of its wing. "And your beloved Remedy, too."

She holds her breath. For a moment, she doubts herself and questions how that could be. Is it true? But how?

"You're a liar," she mumbles.

It stops laughing and assumes an angle of attack. Then it dissolves into nothingness. She feels scared. She feels angry. She feels tired. She chooses not to move, but instead, closes her eyes tightly and ignores the stranger.

"Nothing is real," she says to herself. "Why keep trying when nothing is real? I'm trapped in a cage, unable to fly. Why do I try?"

Massaging Dane's scalp, running her fingers through his silky curls, she reminds herself that Dane is real. His love and the miracle of feeling in love is real. She never imagined that she could feel as alive as he makes her feel. Melting from one arresting kiss.

But she knows that nothing good stays long. Tears fall fast from her squeezed shut eyes. She begins to anxiously nibble on her fingernails. Her mind shifts to Remedy's words that rang out in the thunder.

She meditates on the meaning of her mission, uncertain of exactly what that mission is. She tries to accept the truth, that she is a Warrior – the Fire, and that Remedy is the Roc, from the Kagawi legend. She whispers to herself,

"How is it that what's real and good feels fake, and what seems impossible, no matter how terrifying, becomes reality?"

She feels herself drifting into unconsciousness. "Just rest ... all I want is rest." Images flash in her mind of both the great white owl, and of the six-winged giant flying over water.

Deeply sleeping for what feels like mere seconds, she is awakened by the heinous sound of flapping and buzzing. Opening her eyes, she discovers that Dane has been dragged away from her, across the water to the dark recesses of the cave.

A streak of black oil in the water leads to a cape of black leather draping over Dane's upper body. She watches for a moment while she gets her senses together, then yells out when she sees Dane's legs deflating,

"No! NO!"

She gets up and desperately swims across towards Dane.

The leather cape whips off from his lifeless body. It blows a fierce breeze causing Mercy to take in unnatural breaths through her throat. She stops, and observes the man-sized bat lingering low in levitation over Dane. Dane's body is flat and there is a small hole in his temple.

A hummingbird, made of rhodium, buzzes from the darkness, accompanying the bat. It was the hummingbird's long bill that drilled that hole in Dane's head to slurp out his life. Now all that remains, is a hollow image of what Dane was.

Mercy sprints through the shallow water leading up to the sandy ground. She throws punches at the creatures, but before she can make contact, they turn invisible. She only strikes air. She hears the buzzing wings of the hummingbird, and the reminiscent obnoxious laugh of the bat, fade into the distance. A subtle sonic boom follows, and perpetual thunder begins to break the air outside the cave.

A once tenacious warrior, now a barren queen without her crown.

"I'm sorry, Dane! I'm so sorry."

She crumbles at his feet and moans in angry agony.

"I didn't mean to close my eyes," she sobs, "I didn't mean it. I'm sorry … I'm so weak."

She crawls up against his flattened body, and presses her face against his. She snuggles the body, placing his limp arm around her. She weeps hard, until her head feels like it will explode. Feeling like she will suffocate from her constricted sinus cavity, she sits up abruptly to catch her breath. She squeezes her head to relieve some pressure.

More tears smother her cheeks when she looks at Dane's handsome face. His copper-colored eyes don't shine anymore. He was good … and now, he's gone. She lifts his hollow shell and hugs it tightly.

Rocking back and forth with it securely in her arms, she begins laughing hysterically,

"Oh wow! This is crazy, Dane, isn't it? Who else but me could this happen to?"

She wipes her tears on his once muscular shoulders.

"If Doc was alive, he'd give me a pep-talk about staying awake in critical times. And Rem, oh boy, she would be overloading me with all kinds of motivational stuff."

Dane's head crops to the side from her body movement. Mercy puts her ear to his cold lips,

"What's that, Dane? What did you say?"

She listens silently, then nods her head in agreement,

"I KNEW you would say that! See, that's why I love you. No lectures, no speeches. You just get to the point. You're right, I think we should get into the water, too. It's safe there. Even though it's moving faster into the dark mouth of the cave, it's our best option. What else do we have to lose, right?"

She laughs awkwardly again to herself. With her arms

wrapped around the corpse, she enters the travelling pool.

The current instantaneously pulls them into the darkness. While drifting in the caliginous cove, all that glows are Mercy's eyes. She glances back at the distant bouncing lights, realizing she forever leaves behind an irreplaceable moment.

Holding on to Dane's lifeless body with all her might, she feels the current get stronger. The tidal motion becomes untamed, and she realizes that another unnerving waterfall awaits their inevitable arrival. She hears the surging waves draining out, and imagines a gruesome struggle to survive once she finally tumbles into the furious downpour.

Suddenly, the water swings upwards. It rolls up in fast motion, defying gravity. Mercy and her hollow-man are pulled up, plunging into a reversed waterfall.

Falling up, twisting and turning as if in a tornado, she holds on to Dane, the last bit of reality she has. She angrily pounds the water with her feet in an effort to gain some type of control. Becoming exhausted, she thinks,

"I can't. I'm too tired to fight anymore. I don't have enough energy to do this. Why am I still trying? It's too late anyway. Just let go."

In a split second, she stops all effort, releasing her control to the tugging elements. Just then, she and Dane's shell land on a soft, warm substance still in pitch darkness. She hears the standing waterfall skip farther away from them until she can't hear it anymore.

She lies the corpse on her lap as she sits there. She speaks aloud to him, as if he will answer,

"Where are we now, Dane? It's so dark, I can't see anything."

Just then, a blue light shines forth from above, revealing a valley of black snow. The round blue moon floats in an oddly white, triangular sky, giving light like the midday sun.

She observes neon pink lenticular clouds streaming the celestial triangle. Emerald stars stud the sky, twinkling against the white backdrop of the heavens. The white stratosphere prevents Mercy from discerning whether it is night or day here ... wherever *here* is.

The thick, black snow is warm to the touch. She scoops up a hand-full and smells it,

"Smells like fresh lemons."

She bites a pinch,

"Ah, Dane, it tastes like lemons, too!"

She takes another bite, chewing on the soft, lemon flavored black snow. She rubs the snow residue from her hands, and deftly moves Dane on to the snow to stand up. Overlooking the vast expanse of the deep valley, she notices that nothing makes a sound. Everything is silent.

The phenome of erect waterfalls that surround the valley remind her of immovable steel pillars. They flow up into the triangle sky, while tiny purple snowflakes fall from it. They pop like bubbles mid-air, releasing lemon scented crumbs that fall heavily but disintegrate upon reaching the ground.

"Ok, so I guess we're here. But where is here?" She

nibbles on her thumbnail, "And what do we do now?"

A shadow in the distance catches her attention. It looks like a silhouette of a small hill. She examines the other side of the land for any other solitary hills, but there are none. When returning her glance to the shadow, it has moved considerably closer to her. Then two round, yellow beams shine forth from the shadowy hill.

It sees Mercy, still and curious, watching her nibble on her fingernail. It takes a mental snapshot of her face through its magnified perspective. Transitioning its pleated, comb-like structure of blood vessels in its eyes, it captures her essence in its memory; then disappears.

Aware that her six-winged, yellow-eyed stalker has made it here with her, Mercy anxiously searches for a way to make her next move.

Lightning crashes down in the near distance at a point of movement in the deep snow. At that location, Mercy sees an eight-headed scorpion, the size of a horse, rapidly swim up out of the snow. Its tail pops up as the rest of its body dives back under the snow.

Lightning illuminates the area and thunder rumbles. She sees that the tail curls around a flickering piece of metal, and Mercy instantly knows it's the sword she needs,

"The sword of truth! Dane, I've got to get it."

She looks down admiringly at Dane's body,

"Now you stay right here. I'll be back, I promise."

She caresses his cheek, then kisses his stale ear near the drilled hole left by the hummingbird. She smells his hair which has absorbed the lemon aroma of the popping purple snowflakes. For a second, she hesitates to abandon Dane to move on, but once the thunder vibrates the entire snowy valley, she recalls the conclusion of the Kagawa legend:

For the warrior's salvation, put on the helmet and capture the sword of truth. When the battle begins, again, the warrior will conquer – the Fire led by Roc in flowing Water.

That reassures her that everything will return to normal if she just finishes the mission. It **has to** return to normal.

Mercy treks through the snow as fast as she can in the direction of the eight-headed scorpion. She sees the leviathan wiggling the sword farther away, diving in and out of the snow. Pushing her weight through the blanket of powder, she senses an eerie presence behind her in the silence of the valley.

She looks back, but sees nothing. She knows it's the six winged, whale-headed stalker who creeps closely behind, watching ... waiting.

When she reaches the spot where the scorpion was, the snow begins to crack open from deep within the earth. She jumps back a few steps, until the opening stops at the tip of her toes. Water now fills the earth in front of her, silently wrinkling up and down until it freezes into a thin layer of black ice. Mercy stands on the brink of sleet, looking down into darkness.

She looks back in Dane's direction, but he is too far to see now. She looks down again at the taunting black ice, and takes a deep breath, preparing to embark on the rest of this journey alone. Her reflection stares back at her with its bright red eyes. The image slowly starts turning upside down. She hears a faint flapping sound from the sky, daring her to jump in and end it all.

CHAPTER 7

TO END IT ALL

"Ok, Mer," saying to herself, "You can do this. All you have to do is catch up to the scorpion and get the sword. And once you do, it will all somehow work out. Somehow – it will. You can do it ... you've been through worse than this."

She takes another deep breath, closes her eyes, and jumps feet first into the water. She crashes through the bruising current, like smashing through a glass wall. To her surprise, it is very cold, unlike the warm snow above. Ironically, the cold burns her accelerating body with the precision of razor blade slices, and stabs her face like needle pricks.

Freezing water ruthlessly swallows her down. Her heart momentarily stops, adjusting to the dramatic temperature. Puffing in and out frosty bubbles under water, she begins sinking like a block of frozen cement, numb with frost bite.

Disoriented from the force of impact and freezing

water, she wildly attempts to swim back up to the surface, her arms and legs involuntarily paddling. Once she realizes she is swimming deeper, upside down instead of rising to the surface, she panics. On impulse, she frantically breathes in, and feels her lungs begin to fill with water. She gathers the strength to flip herself around, planning to swim up. But her muscles weaken and her bones shiver uncontrollably, and she can't move.

As she floats in a delusional condition, she feels the ominous presence of the winged assassins nearby. She looks up to the surface and sees a giant blurry shadow recklessly hovering in the air above. It rocks with the movement of the underwater current, heaving with intensity.

Growing larger, it ferociously tracks where she is underneath. She uses all her strength to swim to the right but the shadow above patterns her every move. Her reality becomes that she cannot escape no matter what she does or how hard she tries. Paranoia sets in,

"They're everywhere! Either way, they're gonna get me."

Her depleting air supply leaves her hopeless to the prospect of survival, let alone at retrieving the sword from the thieving scorpion. She waits. The more time that passes, the more she realizes that the shadow above will not leave until it gets her. She waits in agonizing anticipation for the unthinkable attack from above. She waits...

She feels the light in her eyes dimming; the life leaving her body. Then the inevitable happens: the shadow figure bashes through the freezing liquid grave, seeping like oil straight towards her. She waits expectantly for her bleak defeat.

Focused on the arrival of the shadow, Mercy doesn't see the furry white image scrupulously emerging from the depths of the descending ocean below her. It swims behind her with its two big glowing eyes and reaches out a strong arm. Without yet seeing it, Mercy feels the sticky black footpads on the giant paw reel her to its warm body. Its barbwire claws gently hold her in place.

She feels conflicted, weary of whether this creature will help or harm her. But she has no strength left to resist. She chooses to give in and trust it.

It bends its head over her and touches her nose with its nose. Mercy hears it make a low humming sound, a response to stress that a mother bear makes when worried for her cub's safety. Its pure white fur floats all around like tall blades of grass swaying in the wind.

Hundreds of fur strands pluck off its coat, and float towards Mercy's face. They strategically arrange themselves around her head, forming a helmet. Simultaneously, the creature generously blows oxygen into the furry helmet, and continues to wrap her in a hug with gentle pressure.

Mercy breathes in the helmet's oxygen. She coughs out excess water, which the fur helmet absorbs. She feels warmth from the compassionate beast's body bringing insurmountable life back to hers. It helps her regain and conserve energy, so that she recalls her own strength.

The gentle giant releases her from its grip, and the little strands of fur remove themselves from around Mercy's head to return to their source. The creature orbits around her, displaying its tremendous size and astounding beauty.

She knows that it understands her rejuvenation, and intends to leave her now that she feels better. She shakes her head *no* at it; demanding it not to leave. It waves its paws, impervious to her plead for it to stay, and gradually fades back into the darker part of the water, out of sight.

When she looks back, she sees that the massive black cloud from above has already reached her. Caught off guard, she screams out. The pressure of her remarkable scream creates a concussive blast that shocks the underwater current and vacuums time. Everything stops, except for Mercy.

Thanks to the halted time, she can see the hordes of individual birds that she couldn't see before when they blended together in their nefarious trip towards her. She is calm now, knowing she is in control. Her body moves effortlessly through the water as if being pushed by a strong gust of wind.

She floats towards the stagnant, Nephilim-sized leader bird of the army that intended to seize her. It leads a military of ravens with twisted beaks, that are suspended in a V-shape formation. She gets just inches from the leader's face, and observes the frightful sight.

Its orange eyes leer at her face with aggravation. Its elongated, bright blue fleshy neck carries a wine-red head and razor-sharp beak. Strands of long black human-like hair cover its round body instead of feathers, which waft in the still water. The peculiar stone crest on top its head remains stiff like the time. Its whopping legs end in machete talons.

Each talon carries something of interest to Mercy's mission. The left talon pierces through two severed scorpion heads, while the right holds the sword. This lets her know that she will have one less battle to worry about since the scorpion is dead. It also gives her relief that the sword, what she needs, has coincidentally come to her.

While time remains as frozen as the temperature, she paddles carefully near the giant fowl. It continues to stare forward in the place she moved from. She wrenches the sword from its powerful claw, and urgently swims through the barricade of twisted-beaked ravens.

Their shiny feathers pleat tightly together appearing as a cohesive black steel coat of defense for each raven. Passing their faces, she can't help but notice how their malice beaks create the illusion of gas-masks. Their eyes lock straight ahead in the same direction as their leader, in the place where Mercy was.

Advancing between them towards the surface, she senses the lapsing rate of time. She clenches the heavy sword and begins to swim faster, passing the last of the militant ravens. She so happens to look at one of the creature's eyes as she passes his face.

Its eyes jerk at hers out of nowhere, scaring her to the core. Her loss of self-control causes the troop to begin resuming movement. The raven's head twists back to watch her swim away.

A ray of blue light appears as she gets closer to the surface, chipping away at the blackness embedding her. By the time she reaches the vertex of the water, the ravens and their leader steadily release from the hold of her time-stopping ocular scream. They all turn around after her in a power- take-off.

Mercy manages to use the sword as a climbing device out of the frozen lake. She rolls onto the warm snow. Her followers shoot up out of the blistering water. The leader plops in front of her and snatches the sword from her grip. The army of twisted beaked ravens pour over her, digging their claws into her skin to raise her off the ground.

She feels herself become airborne in their grasp, speeding through the air. The ravens fly faster and faster over the snow, digging their pointed claws into her body, cawing loudly and pecking at her the whole way. Finally, they drop her in the snow next to Dane's body, which they've mangled even more during her absence under water.

All the ravens slew around her, watching her rush to Dane's ruined corpse in complete dismay. She does not care about the malevolent birds or the illogical mission anymore.

"DANE!" she shrieks.

They further ripped his muscles and hollowed bones during her quest for the sword. His haunting copper-colored eyes have been slashed out, as if they did not want his innocent stare cursing their behavior.

She kisses his sandpaper lips, then cries out with excruciating pain, feeling fire from within eroding her breastplate. The arrogant predators watch apathetically.

She begins to moan in a prison of emotional destitute,

"It wasn't supposed to be like this! This wasn't the ending to the legend! It was all supposed to be okay."

Resting her head on Dane's torn chest, she mumbles under her breath,

"First, I lost my best friend, and now I've lost my heart. It's all in vain. Nothing even matters. Why did I do all this? Why? What's it all for?"

Exasperated, she lifts her head and yells directly at the birds,

"**IS *THIS* WHAT YOU WANTED**? Death and loss? Execution and distress? Then you got it – you won. I'm not unbreakable ... I'm broken."

She looks up to the triangle sky,

"But I'm not angry ... I'm not sad ... I'm not anything ... anymore, except alone. Whoever said that the good guy always wins is a DAMN liar! I'm in hell, feeling this way - defenseless against my own emotions. I just want to feel happy. That's all I've ever wanted. Is that too much to ask for?"

Sulking, she stares at the sword in the leader's talon, tempted by its double-edged blade and perfectly pointed tip. The giant leader steps on the sword with his detrimental boot claw to keep her from obtaining it, as if it knows what her thoughts are. The ravens open their twisted beaks mockingly.

Mercy folds over Dane's body, feeling her desire to live deteriorating. Once again, she let Dane down ... she feels like a failure no matter how hard she tries to do good. She disbands in tears that can't seem to drop from her eyes. Her stomach feels nauseous, esophagus raw, and head throbs. For the first time, she feels alive – and realizes how much it hurts to feel alive.

Thunder pops and the Northern lights weave between the stars. She scowls at the birds,

"So ... what are you waiting for? I'm sure you've been ordered to finish off Mercy, too. Go ahead."

They caw in response, cocking their heads, staring

blankly at her.

"DON'T IGNORE ME!" she shouts, spewing foam from her indignant lips.

She moves quickly and yanks the sword out from under the heavy foot of the goliath bird with astounding strength. She attempts to jab it into her own heart, but her breastplate ricochets the intended incision. The bird charges at her, aiming its sharp talons at the sword.

It crushes the remnants of Dane's shredded carcass as it stampedes at her, blotting out any existence of Dane. The crushed matter sifts into the wind like blown chaff. She tastes the sweetness he left on her lips as she watches him fly away ... she never got to say goodbye.

Provoked to pure anger at its disrespect for the little bit of proof she had left that love exists, Mercy thrusts the weapon at the fowl's legs. It jumps over her thrust. She immediately swings the sword around at its head, but the stone crest deflects it. The bird pauses and shoots her an agitated glare.

It turns its back on her. Mercy sees the long black hair

on its back separate, showcasing fossilized diamond-shaped quails on its spine. The quails rub together to create clicking whistles. Mercy observes the clicking quails until the creature blurs into invisibility.

At that moment, Mercy hears a close sonic boom, which blows out her hearing capability. She quickly slaps one of her ears with her free hand, endeavoring to recover her auditory range, but to no avail.

All the perverted-beaked ravens spread their wings so wide that their feathers separate like fingers. Plumage begins to fall from nowhere, covering the snow. Various fowl species spring up from the fallen feathers, and join in with the ravens. Then they all blur together into invisibility.

Knowing what that means, Mercy starts uncontrollably swinging the sword around her like a crazy person. The instinctive will to survive outweighs her desire to give up. As she spins amuck, a fortress of red and black flames sparks out of the sword, encapsulating her.

In a storm of rage, as the flames rise higher, she screams insanely,

"I can't take it anymore! I don't want to be the one who always has to fight just to lose. No matter what I do, it's never good enough. The constant, non-stop, tormenting battle of not surrendering. Test after test. Obstacle after obstacle. Expected to smile and take it all with positivity.

"I'm tired of hanging on. Putting a smile on my face day after day, as if I wasn't crying the night before in hopelessness. As if the deep-rooted, permanent sadness isn't eating out my heart or eroding my mind, making me sick to my stomach.

"Everything good has been snatched away from me. What else is there to hold on to? I was born guilty, inheriting the tears that came before me. Still-born out of a faceless womb, with atrophying optimism. As an innocent child, I would repeat, 'If only I had wings to fly away, like a silent dove to a safe place; then I'd be free.' "

Physically worn down, she stands still now, chopping the sword at nothing. She continues venting out,

"Restless, running for no reason. I crave peace ... not feeling anxiously insecure from my traumas. Instead

152

of feeling lonely, rejected and abandoned. Instead of feeling like I carry all my weight alone, without a break. Wanting to accept love instead of allowing dejection to prevent me from feeling good. Destroying my own inner world because of lack of clarity, loss of purpose.

"I'm locked up like a prisoner in my own soul. Crushed without a helper because I turn people into enemies in my mind, simply because they can live happily past my pain. Trying to catch my breath using claustrophobic lungs and a smashed chest cavity. Fearing waking up tomorrow because happiness experienced today might not reappear ever again.

"My darkest nights remind me that goodness is concealed from me. That there's nowhere to run. That nobody really understands or wants to hear me. That nobody can take this pain away. That a caged animal never grows to its full potential."

She screams at the sky, "JUST LET ME GO! WHY WON'T YOU JUST **LET - ME - GO**? I don't want to do this anymore! I don't want to be alone anymore!"

She looks into the sword at her reflection. Tears of blood leave tracks on her cheeks.

"This is me. This is really me … this is all I am. This is it."

She throws down the sword and looks around herself. Fascinated by the fire wall encircling her, the thought occurs that she might not be as weak as she allows herself to believe. She looks up, beyond the wall that she created, at the triangle sky.

She feels thunder beating harmoniously with the brilliance of the smoky Northern lights that dance with the neon clouds. Another sonic boom opens her eardrums. Clumps of thick, hot wax ooze out of her ears like honey.

She feels a hard rumble and sees the triangle sky split open with a loud cracking sound. The majestic white owl swoops out from the opening.

It glides in the air, whooshing within the clouds, making a whistling sound that matches the quail clicks of the invisible leader bird standing on the other side of Mercy's fire wall. The owl travels to one corner of the triangle sky and unzips one edge completely.

Out from the unzipped edge of the sky, a flying

specimen, shining with shimmering stars, slips through the opening and descends at Mercy. She observes it descending at her. Each splendid star in its place forming a dragon shaped body.

Gold eagle wings glisten. A multi-colored peacock tail trails behind, sweeping over the other stars. Though it is faceless, Mercy sees a beak exposing a set of thorny teeth, and holes above the mouth that flash light when they blink.

It flows like a tidal wave constellation from the heights above. It humbly lowers itself to the land, stirring the wind with its enormous wings as it flows. It finally lands mellifluously outside of Mercy's fire encampment, diffusing her wall with its great, balancing tail.

Crawling up to Mercy's face with its transparent, illuminated body, it makes no sound at all, not even a crinkle in the snow.

Erecting itself, towering over Mercy, it flexes each sharply tapered wing at a time. Its regal composure fathoms Mercy.

"So, you're the sonic boom? The *actual* leader of it all?" Mercy asks.

[CHAPTER 8]

AND START AGAIN

The figure continues to silently flex its lavender scented wings in front of Mercy.

"What's the reason for all of this? Tell me what the meaning is, please. Tell me who I am," Mercy begs.

The star dragon remains silent.

"PLEASE! Please. Stop ignoring me. Just talk to me. I CAN'T TAKE IT anymore! The pressure, the headache, the heartburn. This *must* be the last trial ... I'm not as strong as everyone thinks I am. This is too much for me."

It remains silent. Mercy continues desperately,

"Tell me the truth. Tell me something, please. Teach me the truth about myself ... teach me what I am inside."

It cocks its faceless head to the side.

Mercy surrenders, falling to her knees. Her tears wash over her tears. She moans,

"Wipe my tears. Tell me it's all ok. Don't crush my bones because I'm already crushed. No matter what I do, unhappiness traps me."

She stares at the silent being, hopelessly waiting. When it still doesn't answer, she keeps talking,

"I know I'm distraught. I'm distressed. Maybe a little delusional. I don't know why I'm like this. I don't know how I got this way. It's not my fault ... I don't think.

"Please pay attention to me. Give me a reason to keep going. I don't know anything except that I want to feel happy ... I want to feel loved ... I want to feel safe. Defend me with your obvious power. Save me from myself!"

Mercy quickly covers her face. Blood red tears sneak through the cracks of her fingers. The star dragon lowers its golden wings. Clenching its thorny teeth, it releases an imperial sound. In answer, the man-sized bat rises from the black ice like liquid mercury.

It walks to Mercy holding a hyssop branch in its mouth,

"Here," it leans down and puts its nose in Mercy's palm. Dropping the hyssop in her hand, it continues,

"Take this to purify your heart and clear your ears so that you can receive what you need from her. Don't allow your deep pain to transmute into a hollow reality. Pay attention to how you listen."

Mercy apprehensively takes the small, bushy aromatic plant from the duplicitous bat. It steps away from Mercy, and turns its head at the star dragon as if receiving un-uttered instructions. Hovering above the ground, it quickly pierces Mercy's wrist without warning, pushing the hyssop into her bloodstream.

She feels the invigorating minty injection rush throughout herself. Before her eyes, the bat melts away into thin air. The bitter sweet shrub cleanses her disquieting thoughts, calming her mind and heart.

As this happens, the shapeshifting star dragon tilts its

beak back. Its beak opens wide to reveal rows of spiked teeth. It peels off the outer star dragon attire, shedding it like a snake, unveiling a sublimely breathtaking being.

A polymorphic Kagawi Empress steps out of her cosmic covering. She wears a crown of dragonfly wings encrusted into her skull. Her gazelle shaped head suspends in the atmosphere slightly above her shoulders without a neck. Luminescent white rings replace the area where a neck should be. Her hair, made of long white feathers, rolls in waves behind her, streaming out the calming smells of lavender and myrrh.

She has a human face with a dainty black beak. Her slanted owl eyes emit light with each blink of her bee-winged lashes. Bison-like fur adorns her paradoxical body, which is a non-solid flow of energy in an unblemished feminine form. She carries an ice-bow, an optical phenomenon of light interacting with her ice crystal fingers. She stands strong on her five-toed talons.

The tribal Empress begins speaking to Mercy's thoughts without moving her beak,

160

"You've already learned the legend of Kagawa, but the whole story of your dynasty is this:

"Before the Flying Thunder Chief became the ROC (or Rods Of Condensation), she dwelled in the highest mountain, serving as a protection for all life against the Natas. One day, the Natas convinced humans that the mountain's Dweller should be removed because its purpose was too sacred for earth.

"So, they set the mountain on fire while the Flying Thunder slept. The flames began to erode the Flying Thunder into a solid mass of nitrogen dust. It seemed hopeless, as if the enemies had won.

"But the Bird of Paradise, with its perfect courage, fluttered in between the flames. It consumed the fire completely, rising from the ashes, rescuing the mighty Flying Thunder. Thus, earning the name *Blood of Fire*. The Fire and Roc became inseparable from that point forward.

"Mercy, you are the Kagawi warrior. Blood of Fire is your name, to heal the region beyond Kagawa for all other life on Earth, by absorbing energy in oxidation. You are the fire that can consume completely, once your power is realized and accepted. You rise from the ashes. You wear the jasper stone of a warrior, and the sardius stone of righteousness. You are the other half of Flying Thunder - ROC."

Mercy stands in awe, unable to speak. The Empress, and her authoritative answers amaze Mercy. She literally feels the Empress' answers connecting with her brain sensors and knows it's the truth. Mercy cannot find any words to reply.

Knowing this, the Empress goes on,

"I understand you want to be heard, understood, respected, loved. You want wisdom of the sacred secrets of the human heart. To master the treasures of self-reflection, and to explain the end so that you can begin. Tell me if this is your desire."

Mercy responds without concerted thought,

"I don't know what I desire anymore. I keep fighting for something that I don't even know exists. And I keep holding on to things that eventually leave me. Is anything even important now?"

"Everything is always important in the now, Mercy. Say it out loud, what you truly desire."

After brief meditation, Mercy answers,

"I desire not to feel pain anymore."

The Empress tilts her head, and her ice bow starts to glow,

"You beg for a cure from your pain, and yet your pain is what reveals your cure. You misinterpret the journey of your life as pain. Your journey, with all its emotions, is the only destiny that is real.

"Real destiny is your choice to see what's always been within you. To capture control of yourself. To follow that sense of knowing in the path that leads to where you truly belong. Man-made electrical current has deceived your receptors to believe in shortages and scarcities.

"In reality, external factors do not have the power to depress you or weaken you. Only you can do that to yourself, by letting them inside your head. The key is: do not let them get into your thoughts. And if they do, do not let them stay there."

Mercy quickly asks,

"But why am I here? I mean, the journey has only wounded me, like a bird with clipped wings."

The Empress gently snaps her beak,

"You've always had wings. They're not clipped. You just haven't used them to fly. The higher you are, the better your sight to see the bigger picture more clearly."

She abruptly flashes into invisibility, and transports behind Mercy. Mercy spins around to face her. The sweet, dark aroma of myrrh enters Mercy's nostrils, travels down her throat, and circulates through her blood. She feels a rush of indescribable love flow through her veins.

"Every human has one thing in common," the Empress explains, "they all intrinsically want to fly. All humans have the innate urge to feel weightless in the air, floating free. Each one knows this inner reality, but most would rather believe in the limits of impossibilities, so that they do not have to put in the effort it takes to rise."

She then releases her ice-bow and it floats by itself. It spins a web of molecules as the Empress speaks,

"You asked for knowledge. Let me show you. Everyone and everything has a mission and plays a role, whether they want to believe it or not. But let me forewarn you: answers don't solve problems, they only provide knowledge. Knowledge alone does not solve anything. Silence, breath, peace – these activate solutions. Step on the web," she commands Mercy.

When Mercy delays, the Empress extends her hand and wiggles her ice-crystal fingers at her. She affirms,

"Mercy, thought is just an after-thought. The state of simply being allows one the power to surpass all thought and understanding. Just relax, and be in this moment."

These words resonate with Mercy. She takes the Empress' hand to step onto the web that the ice-bow created. Mercy's body instantly sticks to the web and her mind races with images she cannot stop:

She sits in black nothingness, perched on a floating telephone wire, without any ground in sight beneath her. Her feet and hands strangle the man-made current running through the wire. A multitude of birds fly from out of the darkness to join her perched on the wire. They, too, strangle the wire, attempting to stop the unnatural buzzing energy.

The pressure of the air caves in on Mercy; the universe closes in on her. Black holes begin to bite on the existing darkness. One black hole bites off her head, and spits it onto a fake metal tree branch.

Mercy watches her decapitated body fall. A secret underground tunnel has just appeared below, and her headless body runs into it. The tunnel is filled with seeds of the earth packaged in aluminum containers.

She looks down into the hollow tree trunk of the branch her head sits on, and notices it has no roots. The inside stores the inventory of human DNA and harvested organs.

She hears a loud chirping before a gigantic winged creature emerges from the dark. Its wings create such wind, that it turns the air all around into black water.

The giant creature gobbles up the inventory from the fake tree, including Mercy's head. It flies to a floating branch, one made by nature.

It regurgitates the matter, including Mercy's head, onto the branch. Then it neatly and carefully molds the veins and other matter into a nest. The more defined the nest of veins becomes, the brighter the nest shines in the darkness.

Mercy's breastplate and eyes glow. She begins to choke on the steam exploding from within her.

The tribal Empress presses one of her cold hands over Mercy's eyes and the other on her breastplate to cool her down. She clarifies what Mercy's mind sees,

"You're seeing the black holes of the earth and entire universe generated by the energy of hateful humans. Fake metal trees without roots store the inventory of human DNA and harvested organs. Trees that vibrate with the blood of the innocent. We scratch the codes from their fake trees so they cannot succeed in their path.

"Secret underground tunnels packed with seeds of

chaos from all around the earth, thinking they can destroy nature and rebuild it.

"Polluted skies filled with noise and experimental compounds. Neurotoxins and radiation - alien frequencies that diminish organic neurological connections. Ruined breath, and destructive power.

"Shadowy figures transforming into inanimate objects, plants, animals, and even humans, to destroy what they seek to become. Becoming nothing more than malformed, mechanical earth dwellers, noxious with emptiness, cognitive only of ignorance. Those called the Natas, darken the boundaries of positivity with their processed fluoride and other dangerous components.

"Forcing people to habitually run away from both the self and the other. From reality and true protection. Entrapping people in the caterpillar stage, cocooned and isolated, waiting helplessly for a miraculous transformation into something better. But better never comes because it doesn't exist in the way people expect it to appear."

Still clinging to the web, Mercy asks,

"Who are the Natas?"

The Empress wildly flaps her bee-winged lashes,

"They are whatever negative thing humans invent them to be. The manifestations of anything lacking courage, lacking focus, lacking love. Mind disruptions that seep into the physical world. A negative mind contributes more damage than a material weapon."

Mercy asks,

"And the nest?"

"And finally, a galaxy sized nest made of human veins, white blood cells and selective brain tissue. The regurgitation of life in the land beyond Kagawa, the restoration of the story. The true components needed to exist; the raw materials of existence."

Mercy interrupts with another question,

"Are the birds meant to destroy, like the Natas?"

The Empress fizzles in and out of invisibility. The myriads of birds that previously turned invisible, now flash into vision, then to invisibility again. The bat's voice rings from no specific location,

"Destruction only exists for those already dead."

The Empress reappears directly in front of Mercy's face,

"No, birds are no part of the Natas. The Natas are of an unknown origin. Birds originate from Kagawa.

"Birds hold the authority of sacred secrets because they have seen more than any other creature. They are the *only* ones with the vantage point that sees **everything**, good and bad; from up in the sky, down on the land, or deep in the sea.

"Birds have been entrusted to restore life. De-worming humans of their living codes, in order to regurgitate them into the next earthly era."

Mercy's breastplate begins to sizzle as she listens and meditates on the explanation. Droplets of heat melt through her insides to her back. She feels the web loosening from her steam.

Intrigued to learn how the Empress fits into all of this, she asks,

"And you? Who are you? What's your name?"

The Empress' exotic turquoise-colored owl eyes stare into Mercy's,

"I am *imagination*. A relic of an earlier time. The space between two hemispheres, controlling the portal for realms both seen and unseen. Perception personified. My name, *Se'lah*. Guardian of the enigmatic triangle where life on earth first began."

She warps to Mercy's side, and presses firmly on her breastplate. Her icy touch relaxes Mercy's sweltering body. Her sugary scent stimulates Mercy's taste buds.

"I am you," the Empress continues, "I am them," pointing to the multitudes of birds that blink in and out of visibility.

Just then, the web holding Mercy snaps, and she slams to the ground. Her spine and the back of her head hit the snow so hard that she hears a subtle crack. She lies there for a moment with eyes still closed, talking aloud to herself,

"I can employ my power, which means facing myself and feeling my scars; accepting responsibility for others, and accountability for being me...

"OR ... I can abdicate my power, letting go of any truth to become 'normal,' numb to emotion, and pretend to be unaware of any of this."

She sighs deeply,

"Or ... I could just go to sleep."

She flaps her arms and legs in the warm black snow, inadvertently creating a snow angel. Soon, she doesn't feel the ground anymore. She opens her eyes to see the Empress' ice bow floating underneath her, lifting her up compassionately onto her feet.

When Mercy rises, the Empress grabs her hands and interlocks fingers. She pulls Mercy to herself and hugs her. Their bond releases particles that sync together and erupt into black rose petals. The petals float up between them.

Mercy feels the satin touch of the petals brush against her face. They inhibit the reception of emotional toxicities. The Empress astutely explores Mercy's reaction to the black petals. Mercy keeps silent, but her eyes scream out.

The Empress kneels at Mercy's feet,

"Scars always fade, Mercy." She affectionately grooms the scars left earlier by the fire ants.

She implores,

"You're never alone. Kagawa is your family, and has always been with you. *Kagawa* - made up of the most powerful elements, water and air. All things are anomalies of water. Even air is the highest transfiguration of water. These have always guided you, given life and protection to you. The water that flows within you, and the breath you breathe from all around you.

"Although you feel smothered with worry, and malnourished emotionally, do not be afraid. Despite being inundated with fears and the desire to succumb, believe that you truly are safe. You are equipped with your complete armor, even if it doesn't appear altogether with you in a physical way."

She looks up at Mercy,

"Choose to accept yourself; to embrace who you are in your original Kagawa form. If you do, you will conquer. Self- awareness and gratitude are the only pathways to love and true happiness. Come and see. A warrior must keep fighting to show that *LOVE is greater than pain.* If you forsake your place, you will never see."

The Empress looks up at the Great Owl. It glides in and out of the clouds, making a trifecta of hisses, shrieks and hoots. She looks back at Mercy,

"You only have one chance to choose. And you don't have any more time left with me. Kagawa beckons me to begin the restoration. I am not the final authority – **it** is."

The rhodium hummingbird whips out from within the white feathered mane that erupts from the Empress' skull. It easily drags the giant, dragon shaped star robe to the Empress' talons, and speeds away afterwards. The Empress stands up and the luminescent rings above her shoulders begin to spin, sparking off embers.

Embers from the rings collide with Mercy's breastplate, seeping through its bone and gem layers. Mercy looks down at her breastplate becoming as lava. Light from her blazing eyes synthesize compounds with the lava, raising her temperature to an ethereal degree. She feels these new molecules solidifying in all her organs, and travelling to her back. She lets out an odd moo sound.

Out from invisibility, in answer to her moo sound, walks her whale-headed stalker. It moos and hiccups in reply to her. Then it chomps its thick, fossilized bill a few times. It keeps its round, penetrating yellow eyes on hers. Mercy finally meets her stalker up close, but is unafraid. Its anthropomorphic stare gives it a refined civility, so she no longer feels fear in its presence.

It crouches down. Its knee joints bend backwards, supporting its crouching frame. Inching closer to her staying low to the ground, it makes no sound.

It silently creeps towards her. Finally stopping only

feet away from her, it faces her and erects itself tall.

It throws out its six colossal wings, each pair at a time from its back, and begins flapping. The sound is like cloth flags riotously flapping in the benevolent breeze. Then it stops, retracting each set individually.

Moonlight deflects off its silver coat, creating a silver statue appearance. Standing as stiff as stone, it continues its gaze on Mercy. This time, it doesn't instantaneously disappear like it did all the times before. This time, it remains in front of her, brazen and powerful. And Mercy feels undaunted.

The Empress introduces the bird to Mercy, while stepping inside of her cosmic outer shell,

"Meet your personal watchers," she gestures to the whale-head, as her star dragon robe gulps her down.

When staring at the stalker who stands before her, Mercy notices another creature of the same species slowly leer its whale head out from behind the first one. There are **two** personal watchers over her. The second one's copper-colored eyes sparkle with handsome familiarity. Her breastplate melts faster at the sight of this second watcher.

Mercy drills into its copper-colored eyes, and suddenly tastes sweetness on her lips. Then she realizes the second watcher is Dane! And Doc must be the one in front of him, who has been following her since the beginning! Purple rain falls from the neon clouds, causing steam to rise from Mercy's skin.

The bat's voice abruptly intervenes from the nothingness in a menacing tone,

"Choose Kagawa, like Remedy, and your companions. Become your authentic self like they have, to complete your mission. If not, you will be regurgitated like the rest who will repeatedly start again, until the era finally arrives that will irrevocably deplore the Natas. This is it."

Mercy notices that the Empress is fully clothed again as the star dragon, floating above her. Now, the myriads of birds all maintain constant visibility, waiting for Mercy. The whale-heads watch her intently. The twisted beaked ravens flap their open wings. The fossil-crest on the troop leader's head gleams. The funeral storks clatter, and vultures bob their heads. The man-sized bat grins. And all the other birds look on in anticipation.

Mercy feels hardening sediment moving around within her soul. She feels it seep through the pores on her back, opening her skin from the inside out. She sees her flesh as if for the first time, thin and transparent.

All her cracks show clearly. Her veins flow strong with life, making her flaws appear beautiful. The past is irrelevant now. She reaches around to touch the area on her shoulder blade that leaks a hot, solid substance.

Before she can touch her back, though, flames nip at her hand. But she's unharmed ... because they are her own flames. Pushing her hand deeper into the fire, she feels feathers.

She pulls the fire over her shoulder to see wings layered with rainbow-colored feathers. Radiant wings made alive by the flames, merged together by transient lava. Diamonds adorn the vanes of each wing. The candid valor, belonging only to the Bird of Paradise.

A poetic whisper from the falling purple rain sings in

her ears,

"You want inside the sky at an odd hour, to fly away into the dark of a fire kiss, to end it all and start again."

Mercy wraps herself with her fire rainbow wings like a comforting blanket, exhaling white ash from her nostrils. Then she opens her wings wide, exposing her engulfed body. Reaching out with open palms to the star dragon in front of her, she communicates her final choice by thought.

The star dragon tilts its head at Mercy's decision. In that moment, it aggressively dives in at her, along with all the other birds, shattering the image she used to be.

****

Glass shatters all over the floor near Mercy's bed in the Cognitive Neuroscience Lab. Two scientists hurry to clean up the mess from the broken beaker where her body lies inside a liquid iced chamber, connected to monitoring equipment. Mercy lies unconscious to the outer world, while the outer world is unaware of her inner world.

Over two weeks have passed since the high impact plane crash she died in, passing through Fly Geyser, Nevada. Her body was miraculously the only salvageable one rescued from the mangled scene. In fact, the rescuers found *only* her body on the ruined plane. No other passengers; no pilot or co-pilot. Just Mercy, all alone, without identification of any kind, except for her personal journal and a map to the Bermuda Triangle.

Since no relatives or friends reported a *missing person* alert, neither at the time of the incident or up to 7 days thereafter, the authorities turned her remains over to the local health laboratory for testing and other scientific use. Particularly due to the complex nature of how her body stayed intact despite the crash. Groups of specialized scientists perform various tests in hopes of bringing her back to consciousness.

Top secret, advanced brain and organ preserving equipment keeps her cells functioning. A white ball rises from the bottom of the oxygen tank to pump air through the tubes in her nose and throat. Intravenous solution drips in the triangular pouch hanging above her chamber, leaving trails that resemble white strands of long fur floating underneath a calm current.

Heated electrodes attach to her pressure points from scalp to toes, recording neurotransmission and anatomic motion. Precious stones spin inside the drilled tubes welded into her chest, piercing her heart. The spinning stones mimic a natural electric current pushing her lukewarm blood through her cold body.

Mercy's rubbery skin rests on soft black sheets, cold air blowing all around her, pushing her red strands of hair around like a moving fire. Neuroscientists, psychiatrists, and gene therapists surround her, standing over her chamber like steel pillars of water. They carefully observe her and record the data on the brain image scanners.

"These results are baffling," says the lead neuroscientist with crossed arms in disbelief.

"Her right brain hemisphere is blazingly active, despite her being clinically dead."

A psychiatrist adds,

"Which makes sense, since the right brain hemisphere controls fantasy oriented thinking, and her journal proves this must have been her most dominant frame of mind at the time of death. Her journal is filled with various characters, maps of unknown worlds - apparently inside the Bermuda Triangle, scripts of ancient mystical legends, and random poems.

"She frequently scribbles a poem by Langston Hughes, on almost every page, called 'Suicide's Note.' It reads:

"The calm, Cool face of the river, Asked me for a kiss.

"To which she adds her own poetic words:

"It knows I'm fighting, Exhausted, Needing a Release.

"Poor girl, sad and lonely. She seemed to have had a battle in her mind, with the goal to conquer the sadness at any cost, as if she was a lone warrior. Such a pretty, obviously resilient young woman, all alone. We don't even know her name."

A gene therapist interjects,

"Although we don't have her name, we have something better: her DNA. Our team found some interesting findings last night that we'd like to share. Our tests were initially meant to identify a nameless girl in a mysterious plane crash, and bring her back to consciousness. Instead, these clinical trials have revealed answers to something we weren't expecting.

"A cure for something that shows up sporadically to wreak havoc on the mind, and then hides. Like an attacker that appears for a moment, then turns invisible. A cure for sadness – *depression*, if you will. It doesn't care how old or young a person is. It attacks viciously and unrelentingly. Lurking invisibly until it finally strikes – again and again.

"Ironically, the very sadness causing anguish, might also be a huge part of the cure. We believe the data finally answers the mysteries of a broken mind suffering from depression, like *how* and *why* some minds begin to negatively attack themselves.

"Would you like to know the pathway and process of a twisted mind? First, let me explain the foundation of our understanding before we can discuss the details."

Pointing to the 3D screen of blood test data, the gene therapist continues,

"A revelation in DNA coding that science has not

183

previously discovered until our project now. This girl's DNA does not match any biological specificity in the human genome. In humans, *only white blood cells* hold personality characteristics and genealogical patterns. But in hers, these also show up in her *red blood cells* ... molecular behavior that only happens in **birds**.

"What's unique to birds besides feathers and wings? Large, strong hearts and hollow bones, which she also has. We found the links to how these physical characteristics directly affect her DNA, and by extension, her mind. If others who have chronic sadness match these same genomic patterns of bird-like DNA, this could reveal new pathways to reshaping our understanding on the definition of both depression AND birds."

All the scientists in the lab listen carefully. They eagerly anticipate more details regarding Mercy's identification, as well as this newly found discovery linking bird-like DNA to how and why depression comes about in certain people's minds. But the genealogist cuts the explanation short, reminding them of their time constraints,

"In just a few short hours from now these machines and chemicals keeping her 'functional,' will automatically shut off, as they can only preserve a corpse for exactly the allotted time she's already reaching. After that, her brain tissue will instantly turn to mush, and her flesh instantaneously decay, melting away as if burned by fire. We should run the last test before we compile and finish discussing these rare findings on what happens in a chronically sad mind...

"Let's administer the new solution to finish our last trial, and be grateful that her mind has given the most effective answers to date in the history of all research on depression. Hopefully, we have found a real remedy, not only for her, but for all other captives battling sadness, imprisoned by their own mind."

The team of gene-therapists prepare the new serum to inject into Mercy. Masked and gloved, they carry a large concealed box from the cooler to the table near Mercy's bed. They open the box by unlatching the side locks. A cool mist slithers out from inside the box when they remove the lid. They proceed to pull out two vinyl bags containing thick purple solution.

The doctor holds up the purple solution,

"A cure for the madness. This will break through the brain barrier, and alter her DNA structure. It will replace her organic DNA with a mutated gene called FLY-2-KGWA. FLY-2-KGWA will modulate cell growth, allowing mutant cells to escape and regrow. It should prolong survival of active receptors by weakening the pathways of gene identification.

"Simply put: We need to first weaken her mental capabilities that are controlled by her blood-line, to ultimately strengthen her mind. The inhibitors in this serum will do that. Her complete living code will be broken down and rebuilt according to the imitation genes that we've pre-programmed.

"Once the life code is broken, she should be alleviated from any trace of who she has always been. We've learned that it is crucial to force adjustments on the genetic level, not just in thought patterns, to eradicate severe sadness. This serum will mimic the pattern that her mind has already practiced during the war of sadness: breaking down to the core, then rebuilding."

They infuse the solution into the I.V. and observe it drip down the tube into her vein. Her body twitches slightly from the minor shock of nitrogen levels peaking. Her heart miraculously beats on its own for several seconds. Within that time, her body temperature flares and breathing accelerates, then returns to normal.

"Look here," the scientist points to the neurofeedback on the imaging scans. "Her cell migrations are perpetually moving south, instead of upwards like they should be. It's as if something physically got into her brain and rewired it in the deepest, darkest regions that control self-worth and purpose."

Mercy's heart beats harder, visibly pounding under her chest. They all pause to appreciate the mesmerizing intrigue of her absence of normality.

The breathing monitor interrupts the silence, beeping loudly from detecting a natural rhythm. Mercy begins breathing slowly, then suddenly starts to choke. Surprised by her response, the physicians rush to her side, open the chamber, and adjust the tubes, shocked at how her lifeless body contradictorily displays so much life. They notice her lower legs and feet beginning to swell, and are seeping out a rancid substance from her pores.

"She's having an allergic reaction," one calls out. "Perhaps the serum targeted the wrong cells."

Blood drips from her closed eyes. Black fog swirls out of her nose and out around her head. The lead doctor motions for everyone to step back,

"What's done is done. If we flush it out now, we won't be able to record the results we need. She doesn't have enough left in her for us to do any more tests. All we can do, is wait."

After a couple of nerve-racking hours pass and no change in Mercy's brain activity, the entire team decides to take a very needed midnight break. Making sure her chamber is locked and neuro-enabling machines are functioning accurately, they leave the room. The door automatically locks, securing itself behind them.

Gathering around the break room table down the hall, they attempt to re-energize for the final phase of observation. They rub their eyes and sip their coffee in stressful silence. The laboratory's unit operator turns up the volume on the desk radio, knowing they need an extra boost of positivity.

"Hey now, hey now. Don't dream it's over…"

The operator sings along shamelessly to the 1980's Crowded House song, lightening up the mood. Looking out of the wall-sized window, one doctor says,

"Look at all the glimmering stars out tonight. It's gorgeous! And look at that! I think it's an owl gliding in the clouds – a big owl, at that."

They all gather at the window to witness the majestic scene. Unexpectedly, a large raven with a twisted-beak slams up against the window out of the darkness. All the physicians jump back from the bird's seemingly premeditated ram into the double-pane glass.

Its jet-black body flies backwards off the glass with its piercing red eyes beaming at them through the window. It disappears out of sight, blending into the darkness.

The alarm begins ringing from Mercy's room, which also startles the doctors. They all look around at each other, thrown off-guard by the strange raven, forgetting for a second what the alarm means. Finally, everyone scuttles back to the room to check on why the alarm went off.

Upon entering, the door automatically closes and locks behind them. They see Mercy's chamber still locked, but inside only flames cover her empty bed. Her unconscious body has somehow disconnected from all the machines.

She's gone.

They all stand in amazement. The lights flicker on and off, and a clinking sound tinkers from inside the wall. In their peripheral vision, a black cape flurries from one side of the wall to the corner vent, then dissolves away. They all look up at the corner ceiling vent, where strands of fire red hair blow through the slots of the vent. Then the power goes out completely.

Once the power generator kicks in, a blue light dimly illuminates the room. This allows them to observe an unseen force suddenly suck the feathered red hair into the vent. The strands vanish.

Then they hear an insanely loud noise unlike anything they've ever heard before. Everyone looks around for the source of the disturbance. Again, a terrifying solitary screech roars out into the air. A series of gurgling caws ensue like a diabolical orchestra. Heavy thumps begin pouncing on the roof.

"It sounds like a hailstorm," one physician mumbles.

"A hailstorm of what? Giant bowling balls?" another asks.

They hear the digital buttons tapping on the access code panel outside of the lab door. The door clicks to unlock. The handle jiggles as the knob turns.

The heavy door creaks while opening slothfully. Each physician scoots up against the back wall beyond Mercy's empty bed, skeptically waiting to see who enters.

A long, sharp bill pokes through the crack of the door bit by bit. Then a colony of heinously massive bodies pushes the door open and steps into the room, showing off the crusty, flaking skin on their featherless heads, and evil smirks engraved in their bills. The doctors all gasp at the sight of the blood-stained creatures that walk in, bellowing throatily to summon others.

Down from above, a half-dozen vultures stomp the roof, falling through the ceiling, screaming with their hooked bills. They land in front of the goliath creatures who summoned them. Their bright red eyes glare at the humans. They begin to bob their burly bodies similarly to how boxers do in a ring when waiting for the start bell.

Crouching down in raptor position, the creatures turn their heads left to right at each other. Their long blood-stained bills clatter powerfully in communication, resembling the sound of wooden baseball bats slamming together.

Nobody moves. Everyone simply looks on with terror in their eyes, sensing looming danger, not knowing what to do.

Finally, the marabou storks stop clattering, and the vultures stop bobbing. All their psychotic, blank eyes fixate on the humans.

Everyone keeps still and silent, until a sonic boom flares out from the night sky, giving a command that only the creatures understand.

In that instant, the birds altogether transfigure into an invisible mob. The scientists scream.

And the great white owl unzips the cotton clouds of the night's starry sky ...

Thank You for reading my imagination!
Until next time...

About the Author

Fiction author AMBER RENEE', writes with the intent to inspire readers to question and imagine. She holds a Bachelor's Degree in English, Writing & Literature; and is also the author of, "Babies Come From Where?!"©2015. She lives with her loving family in Southern California.

Thanks to my family and friends, for always going on my real-life sci-fi adventures with me. *Special Thanks* to my artistic relatives and friends – you know who you are. Your courageous example to open minds using art as the core, both amazes and inspires me. I deeply love you!

Grateful Acknowledgement to the other authors who influence _every_ piece I write. Maybe one day we'll all meet in paradise to create beautiful art together:

Rod Serling – Every scene, every moment, every word becomes life.

Edgar Allan Poe – Master of the enticing short story.

Langston Hughes – One poem dropped the mic, "Suicide's Note."

Walt Whitman – Genius with realistic imagery of fantasy worlds.

Wayne Dyer – An example of powerful intention.

And above all,

The ancient Author and Writers of the Holy Texts
... no words can describe my gratitude
for these sacred writings!

www.ingramcontent.com/pod-product-compliance
Lightning Source LLC
Chambersburg PA
CBHW031107020726
47495CB00007B/2082